Things are just getting started out here, Don. So if you act now, you just might make your escape.
FC AIRPORT
But if you wait too much longer, you're looking at spending the rest of your life out here.
Well, optimistic as always, Captain Bob in the chopper.

Perhaps we'll get some specifics on the next report.

NO COVERAGE.

JUST KEYS.

ENJOY YOUR TRIP, MR. FOOTE.

Candle Light Press
Presents

# The Fairer Sex

## Sex

A Tale of Shades and Angels

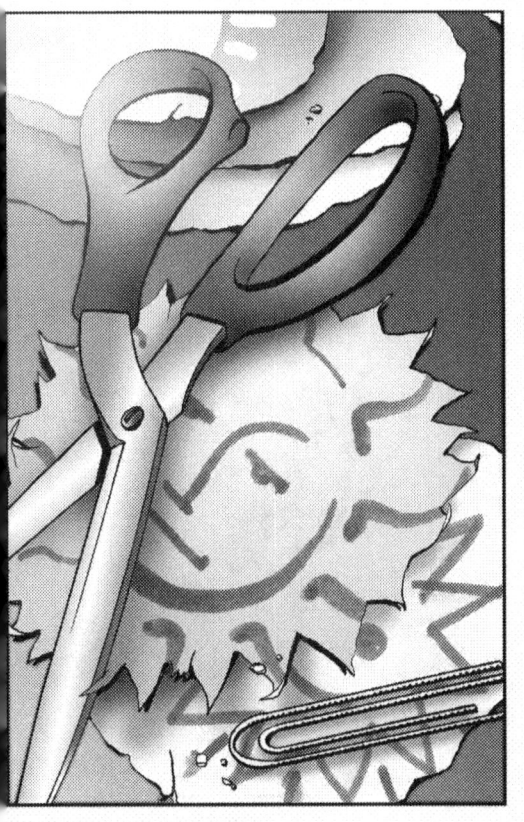

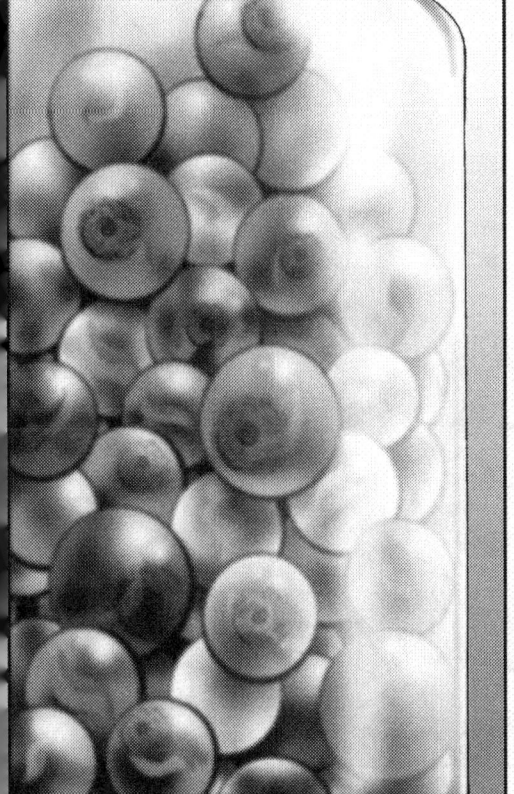
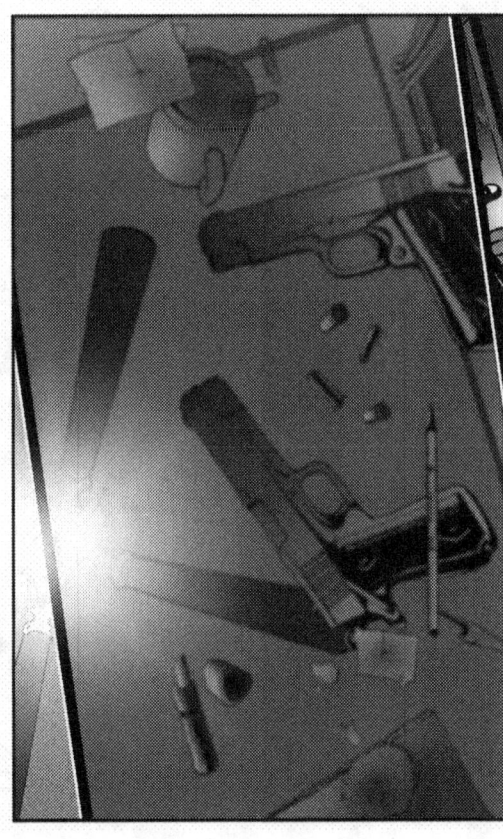

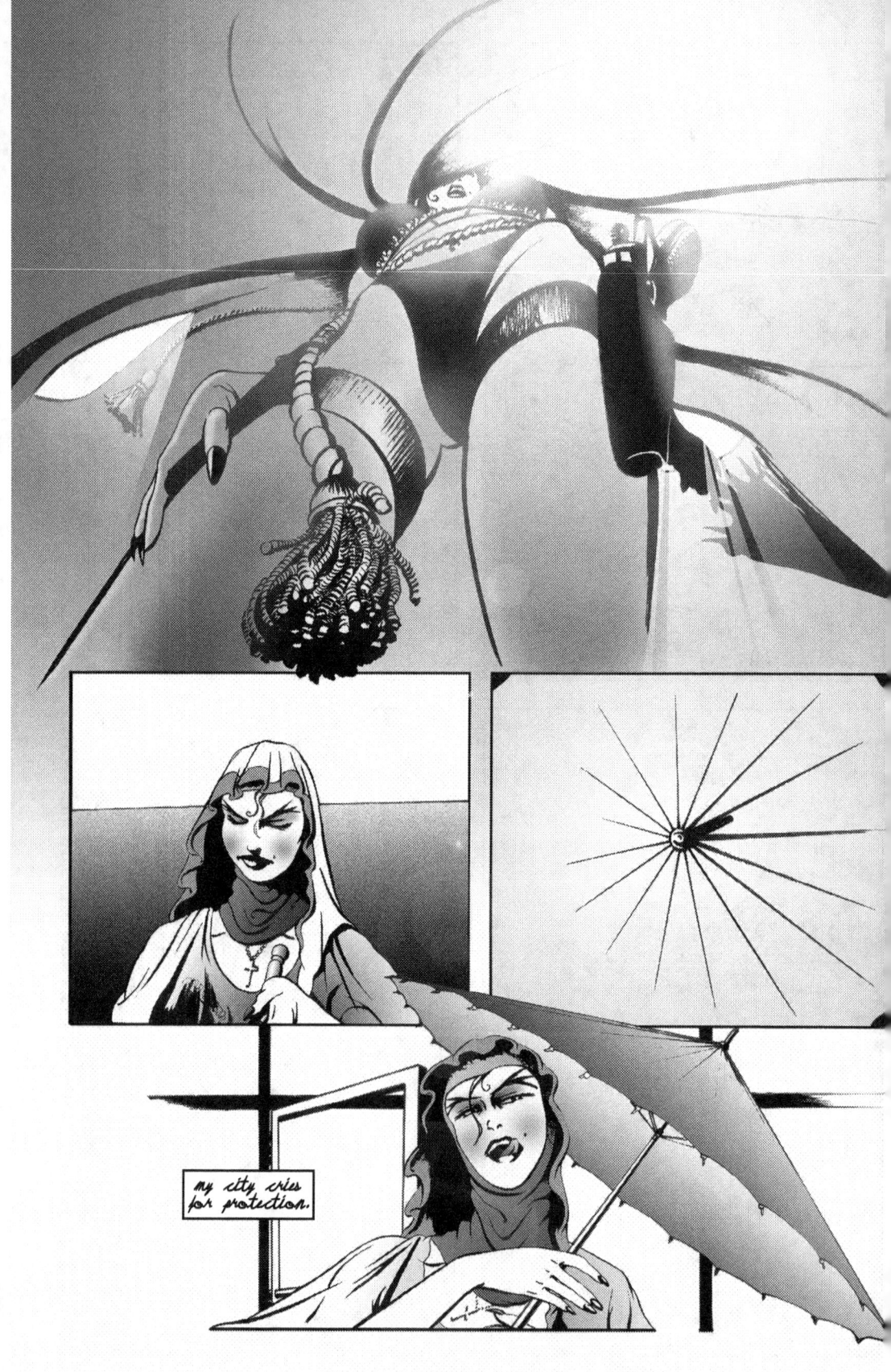

my city cries for protection.

my child inside died for you.

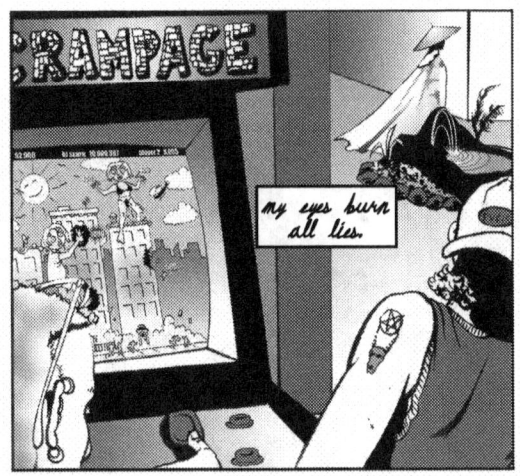

my eyes burn all lies.

i await my love.

i count the moments until he arrives.

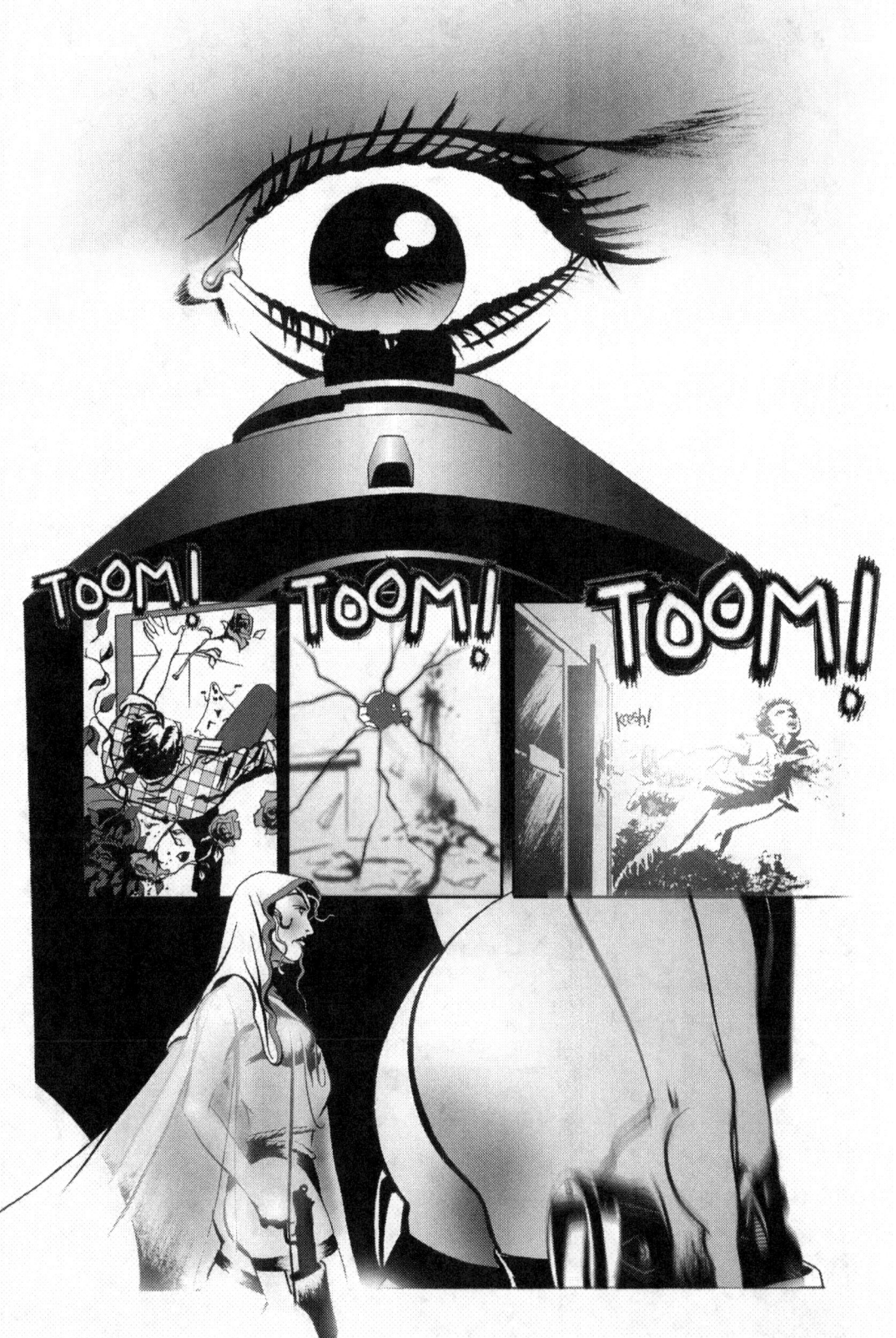

# 1

" 'Mine eyes doth itch; doth that bode weeping?'
'Tis neither here nor there.' "
--Shakespeare, *Othello* IV iii.59

# Scratching An Itch

I'VE BEEN FRED'S PARTNER FOR SIX YEARS, EVER SINCE HE GOT BUMPED, SWAPPED FROM SGT. PEIRCE'S SQUAD...

HANK BERGSON WENT TO PEIRCE, WE GOT FRED.

BEFORE THAT, FRED WAS TEAMED WITH BOB PASTERNAK, A HEAVY-DUTY BLOODHOUND GOING ON THIRTY YEARS IN HOMICIDE...

A LONG TIME TO KEEP YOUR SOLVE PERCENTAGE UP.

BUT BOB SOLVED 'EM, DID WELL, AND WHEN NEWBOY FRED SHOWED UP, HE TRIED NOT TO RUB IT IN TOO MUCH.

THEN SOMETHING CHANGED IN BOB.

THIS SORT OF THING HAPPENS.

GOING ALONG FINE, THEN SUDDENLY YOU WAKE UP AND CAN'T EVEN REMEMBER WHY YOU BOTHERED TO GO TO BED.

A *POSTMAN* WAKES UP WONDERING HOW THE HELL THINGS COULD HAVE GOTTEN *THIS* FAR, SO HE DECIDES TO SHOOT A FEW PEOPLE TO *FORCE* A LITTLE SENSE AND ORDER INTO THE WORLD.

NOT THAT I'M WISHING OR ANYTHING.

NEVER WORKED A POSTAL HOMICIDE MYSELF; FREEDOM CITY HASN'T HAD ONE YET.

I'D JUST LIKE TO ASK THE GUY WHY.

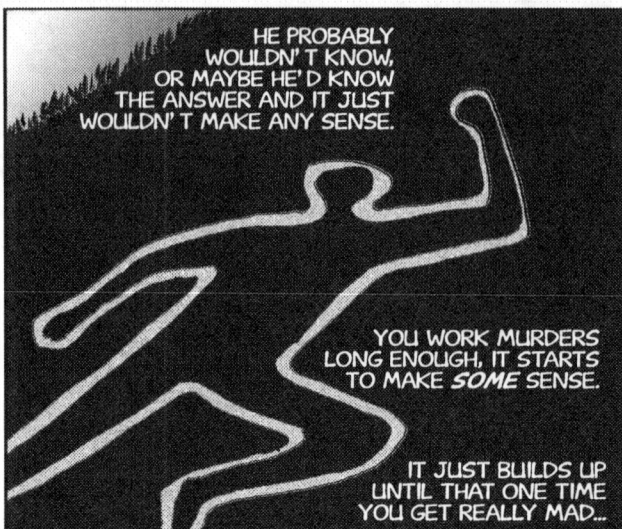

HE PROBABLY WOULDN'T KNOW, OR MAYBE HE'D KNOW THE ANSWER AND IT JUST WOULDN'T MAKE ANY SENSE.

YOU WORK MURDERS LONG ENOUGH, IT STARTS TO MAKE *SOME* SENSE.

IT JUST BUILDS UP UNTIL THAT ONE TIME YOU GET REALLY MAD...

YOU'RE READY TO FREAKIN' CRY OR SOMETHING, AND THEN YOU *IDENTIFY*. YOU SEE IT CLEARLY.

SUDDENLY, YOU'RE LIKE...

YEAH!

I *GET* IT!

THIS IS WHERE YOU SAID *I HAVE TO DO THIS PIECE OF TRASH!!*

YOU *FEEL* IT. AND IF THAT FEELING CAN *PASS*, YOU'RE OKAY. HARROWING OF A PERSONAL HELL, MISSION ACCOMPLISHED. BUT IN BOB'S CASE, IT SHIFTED ALL THE BOUNDARIES, BOBBLED ALL HIS CHECKS AND BALANCES.

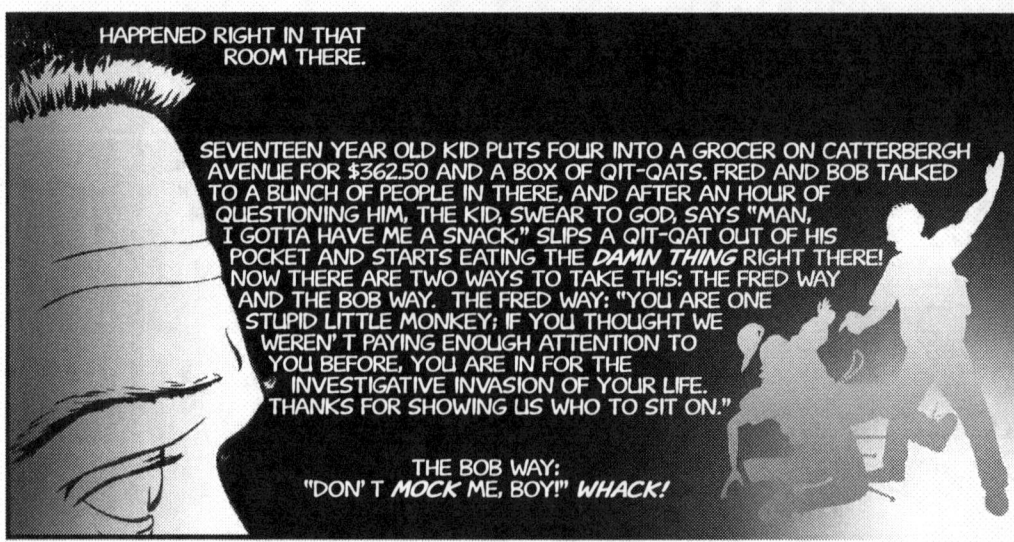

HAPPENED RIGHT IN THAT ROOM THERE.

SEVENTEEN YEAR OLD KID PUTS FOUR INTO A GROCER ON CATTERBERGH AVENUE FOR $362.50 AND A BOX OF QIT-QATS. FRED AND BOB TALKED TO A BUNCH OF PEOPLE IN THERE, AND AFTER AN HOUR OF QUESTIONING HIM, THE KID, SWEAR TO GOD, SAYS "MAN, I GOTTA HAVE ME A SNACK," SLIPS A QIT-QAT OUT OF HIS POCKET AND STARTS EATING THE *DAMN THING* RIGHT THERE! NOW THERE ARE TWO WAYS TO TAKE THIS: THE FRED WAY AND THE BOB WAY. THE FRED WAY: "YOU ARE ONE STUPID LITTLE MONKEY; IF YOU THOUGHT WE WEREN'T PAYING ENOUGH ATTENTION TO YOU BEFORE, YOU ARE IN FOR THE INVESTIGATIVE INVASION OF YOUR LIFE. THANKS FOR SHOWING US WHO TO SIT ON."

THE BOB WAY: "DON'T *MOCK* ME, BOY!" WHACK!

DESPITE WHAT YOU'VE HEARD, LAYING EVEN A FINGER ON A SUSPECT WILL CERTAINLY LAND YOU A FEW MISERABLE SQUIRMING HOURS ON THE WITNESS STAND, BUT 90% OF THE TIME MAKES FOR A BAD ARREST. AFTER THE SMACK, THE KID CONFESSED THE WHOLE THING, EVERY DETAIL. FRED HELPED THE KID UP, WENT TO A PHONE, AND CALLED THE D.A.

FRED SAID THE CASE WAS CLOSED, UNPROSECUTABLE.

THE KID COULD DO HIS CONFESSION IN SKYWRITING NOW AND HIS LAWYER WOULD SAY "AND HE GOT INTO THE BIPLANE AND WROTE THIS IN 50-FOOT LETTERS ACROSS THE WIDE BLUE SKY *AFTER* YOU BITCH-SLAPPED HIM, OR BEFORE?"

I MEAN, WHAT DO YOU *SAY*? FRED SAID PLENTY, BUT ONLY AFTER RELEASING THE KID, ONLY TO BOB, AND ONLY INSIDE THAT ROOM.

EVERYBODY SAW IT, NOBODY HEARD IT.

THREE HOURS, JUST FRED TALKING, YELLING.

BOB WALKED OUT, WENT STRAIGHT DOWN AND PUT IN FOR RETIREMENT.

BUT SGT. PEIRCE WAS LEFT WITH A SITUATION. IF HE DIDN'T DO ANYTHING ABOUT FRED, ALL OF BOB'S PALS IN THE DEPARTMENT WOULD HAVE SKEWERED HIS CAREER, TURNING ALL THE LITTLE SCREWS ON HIM. SO HE VERBALLY REPRIMANDED FRED AND SWAPPED HIM INTO LT. MEAD'S SQUAD...

...WHICH IS NOW DYLAN'S. PAPER MOVED, PEOPLE WERE MORE OR LESS HAPPY.

SO NOW THAT ROOM IS HIS.

NOW *I'M* HIS PARTNER, AND WE *WERE* CHASING THE FEARSOME SHADE. TEN MINUTES AGO, SGT. DYLAN TOOK US OFF THE CLAY TORREZ MURDER.

NINE MINUTES AGO, FRED SUGGESTED THEY HAVE A TALK--IN THERE.

WHAT *IS* ON THE WALLS?

TOK!

PLASTIC PANELING.

DAMN DYLAN, BURYING US IN BODIES.

SEVEN.

HE'S BURIED TOO.

TWOK!

HOMEYS AND PAISANS WENT RAT-A-TAT IN GARDEN GROVE BEFORE WE CHECKED IN.

PROB'LY TWICE AS MANY DEAD.

WHO SAID?

BERGSON.

FIRST SQUAD'S...

MOSTLY STAYIN' TO HELP WITH THAT.

HUH.

WHAT ARE YOU TELLIN ME, HERE?

OKAY, FRED?

DON'T WANNA INTERRUPT THE BROW-BEATIN' OR NOTHIN'...

I WANNA SEE IF I'M THE ONLY ONE BOTHERED BY THIS.

OKAY, LOOK AT THE BODIES THERE.

OKAY, NOW LOOK AT THE SURVIVORS.

BAG OF *WALLETS*.

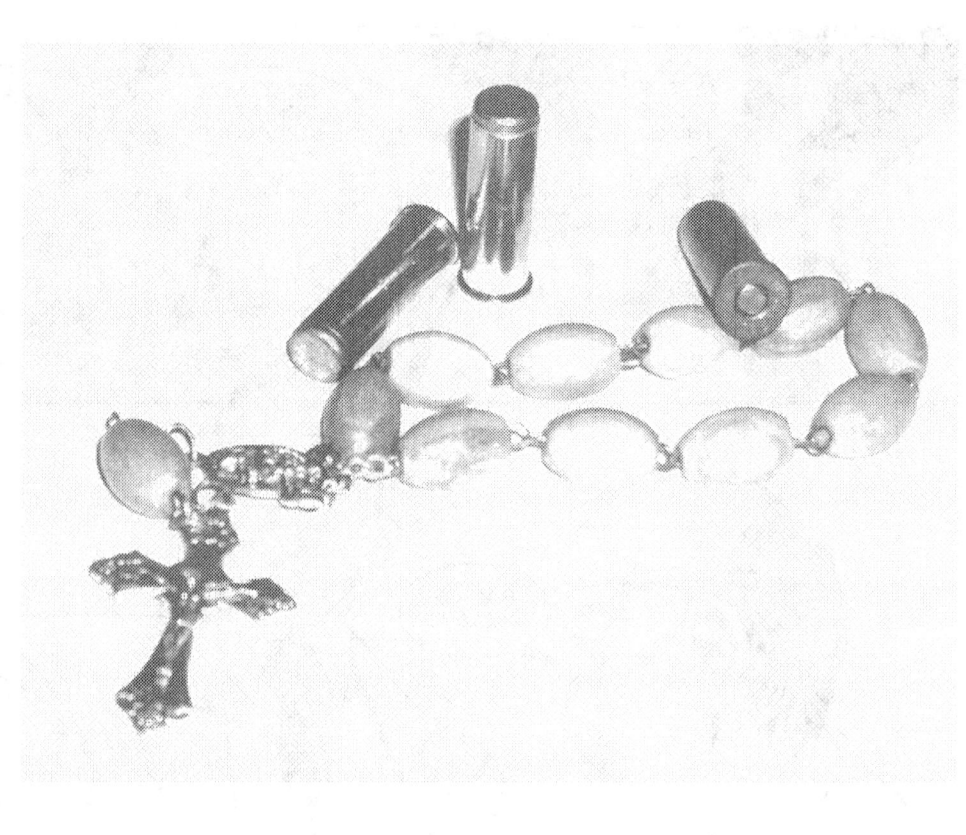

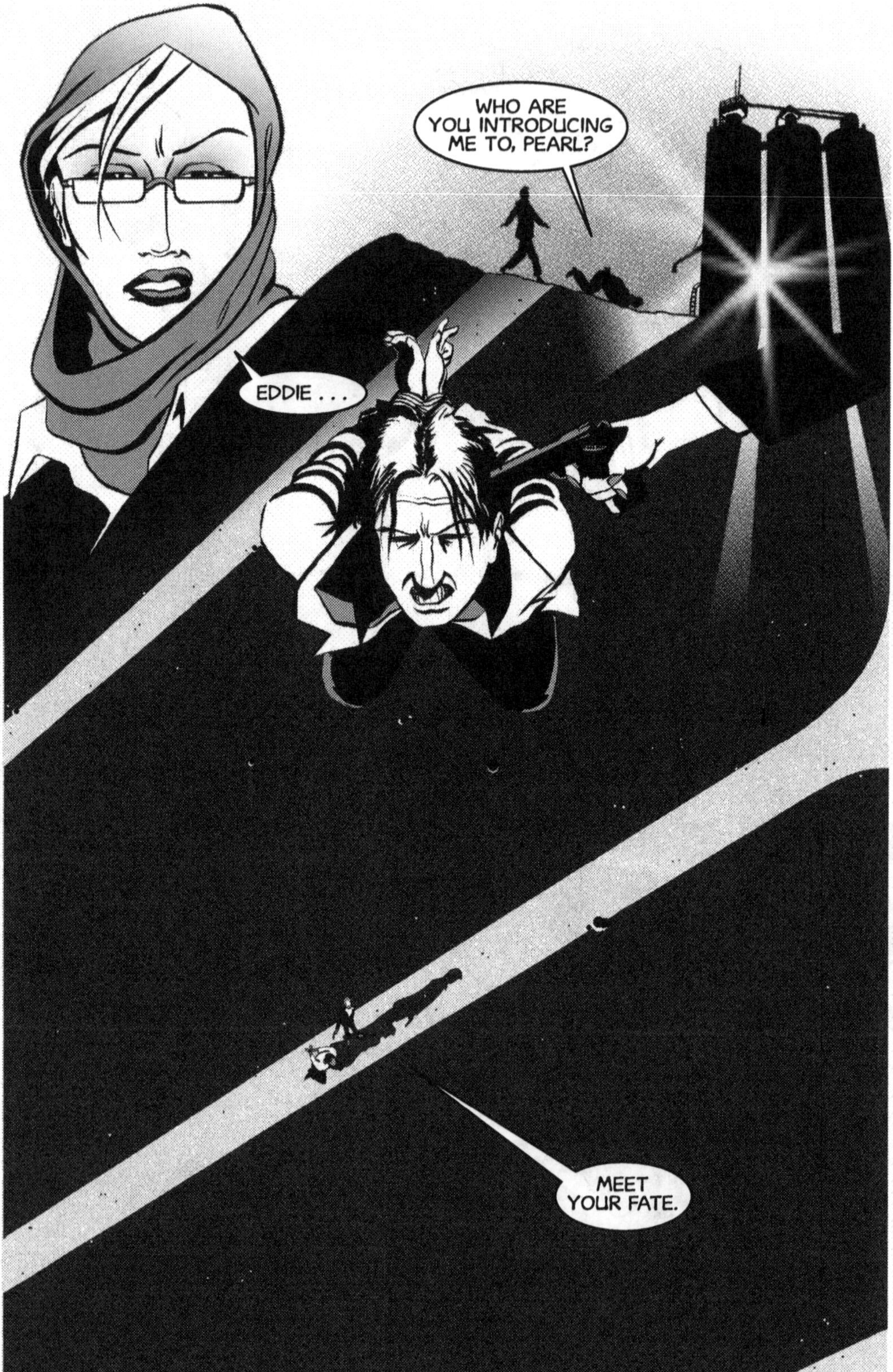
WHO ARE YOU INTRODUCING ME TO, PEARL?
EDDIE . . .
MEET YOUR FATE.

"I hear a voice you cannot hear,
Which says I must not stay;
I see a hand you cannot see,
Which beckons me away."
--Thomas Tickell, *"Colin and Lucy"*

# Rhymes With "Witch" 2

SO WHAT DO WE HAVE?

ONE SHOOTER, REAL TWO-FISTED ANNIE OAKLEY.

CLOSE-QUARTERS SHOTS ARE STRAIGHT.

NUMBER THREE HERE HAS BAM! RIGHT KNEE

AND BAM! LEFT SHOULDER.

EXIT WOUNDS SAY HEAD-ON SHOTS.

SHOTS WITH THE SAME HAND WOULD BE CROSSED UP, AT AN ANGLE.

OTHERWISE, SHE'S SPINNING IN A CIRCLE, AND THEN WE'D HAVE SOMEBODY I'D SUGGEST A SWAT TEAM GO GET.

PLUS, THE SHOOTER'D HAVE TO BE THE O-RIGINAL FLASH TO GET ALL THOSE SHOTS OFF SO CLOSE AND SO VITAL.

SHE A GOOD SHOT?

SHE'S OKAY; KNOWS WHERE TO HIT TO STOP A FELLA: CHEST, HEAD.

I THINK THE KNEE SHOT ON #3'S EITHER EAGERNESS OR OPPORTUNITY.

MOST IMPRESSIVE SHOT'S #11 IN THE LOT OUT THERE.

SHE WASN'T CLOSER FOR THAT?

FROM MY INTERVIEWS, PART TWO OF WHICH YOU ARE INVITED TO STARTING AT SIX THIS PM,

AND THE INTERVIEWS OF OUR PICKPOCKET PALS WITH THE *HATS*. . .

cell's -a- poppin'

american pregnancy

*THESE* ARE WHERE FIVE OF THE WITNESSES WERE STANDING WHEN THE GUNFIRE STARTED.

LINE OF FIRE, SO GOODBYE #7, THEN #9'S IN THE CLEAR.

SHE PICKED 'EM; HAD A PROBLEM WITH SHOOTIN' LADIES,

BUT IT WASN'T NO SURPRISE TO HER.

MADE ADJUSTMENTS THAT TOOK A COUPLE SECONDS.

*DE-FIN-ITE-*LY TWO GUNS.

SO A WOMAN IN A DRESS . . .

WEIRD CRAP DISCOVERED IN INTERVIEWS PART TWO . . .

TWO SAID "WEDDING DRESS", OTHERS SAID THEY DIDN'T GET A GOOD LOOK.

SEVEN WITNESSES DESCRIBE HER AS WEARING SOMETHING LIKE A WHITE NUN'S HABIT OR LOOKING "LIKE MARY". ONE USED THE WORD "GARB".

Susan's

SEVEN OF 'EM DID.

WHAT ABOUT THE LADY WITH THE . . .LOOKED LIKE A WIG?

NO-REETA.

SHE WAS TAKING IT ALL PRETTY WELL.

SHE ALSO CALLED OUR SHOOTER THE "MADONNA". I'LL BE TALKING WITH HER A *LOT* MORE TONIGHT.

NOREETA, WHY ARE YOU STILL HERE?

YOU THINK I GOTS SOMETHING T' TELL YA, FRED. AND I DON'T.

IT'S CLEAR TO ME, *NO*-REETA...

THAT YOU DON'T WANNA BE MUCH HELP TO ME. NOW WHY IS THAT?

MAYBE YOU AIN'T ASKING THE RIGHT QUESTIONS.

AWW, NOREETA.

PHILOSOPHY I CAN GET FROM A *CHINESE* DINNER.

I *NEED* ANSWERS.

JUST GET *USED* TO THE WAY A WOMAN'S MIND WORKS, FRED.

NO SMOKING.

WHAT, ARE YOU GONNA ARREST ME FOR SMOKING?

I AM *REAL* TIRED OF THAT DAMN LINE, NOREETA.

HIT ME WITH ONE OF YOUR OWN *O*-RIGINAL THOUGHTS.

SOMETIMES THINGS GET SAID A LOT 'CAUSE THEY'RE TRUE, OR . . .

THEY MEAN THE SAME IMPORTANT THING TO A LOT OF PEOPLE, FRED.

SHE SAID SHE WAS PROTECTING THE CITY.

FUNNY WAY TO DO THAT. WHAT WAS SHE PROTECTING THE CITY FROM?

CRUELTY, I THINK. AND, AND HATE.

YOU THINK SHE *LOVED* THOSE MEN TO DEATH? WHY JUST THE MEN, CARLA?

ANY THOUGHTS?

SOMETHING THEY'VE DONE, OR SOMETHING THEY ARE. SOME, SOMETHING DIFFERENT...

FROM THE STUFF WE USUALLY THINK ABOUT.

WELL, I HARDLY CON*DONE* MURDER, DETECTIVE, ER . . . HOBBES.

WHY IS IT YOU THINK YOU WEREN'T HARMED, JANINA?

I DON'T KNOW WHY.

YOU STOOD THERE WITH PEOPLE DROPPING DEAD ALL AROUND YOU. YOUR... *PETER*, PETER ALDON.

A MAN WHO WORKED FOR YOU FOR THE BETTER OF TWO YEARS . . .

SHOT DEAD RIGHT THERE.

WHY HIM?

THAT'S . . .

JUST WHAT HAPPENS SOMETIMES.

I'LL TELL YA A STORY, FRED.

IT WAS WHEN I WAS FOURTEEN THAT MY BROTHER RAPED ME.

YUP. NOTHIN' WAS EVER DONE.

NOT BY YOU?

NOBODY.

'N' WHEN THEY BURIED HIM, HIS SON CALLED ME JUST THIS WEEK TO ASK IF I NEEDED A RIDE TO HIS FUN'RAL.

I SAID THERE WAS NO WAY I'SE GOIN' TO *HIS* FUNERAL.

SEE HIM GET PUT DOWN; PUT SOME KIND OF ENDING TO THE MEMORY.

NO POINT, FRED. I KNOW HE'S GONE. DON'T HATE HIM ANY LESS, DON'T LOVE MYSELF ANY *MORE*.

SO I GET SENT A PICTURE OF MY BROTHER IN THAT COFFIN, AND HE'S HOLDIN' A PICTURE.

I'SUME IT'S HIS WIFE.

BUT MY DAUGHTER PUTS A MAGNIFIER TO IT AND SAYS

"THAT'S A PICTURE OF YOU, MOMMA."

'N IT WAS.

TAKIN' YOU WITH HIM.

OH, HE TOOK ME, ALL RIGHT.

'N I DON'T GET IT BACK. EVER.

'S A SAD STORY, NOREETA. SAD STORY.

FUH.

IT JUST HAPPENS. IT'S MAY AND HE JUST COMES...

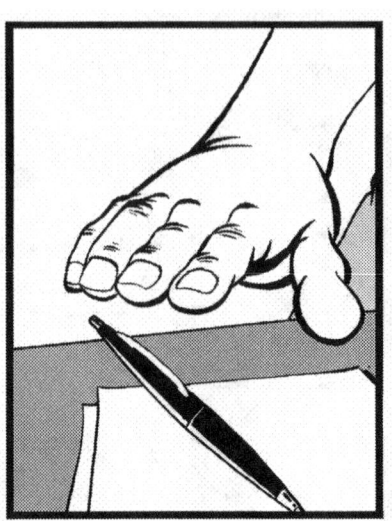

BEFORE WE GO ON, YOU BETTER TAKE A STATEMENT.

SHE JUST TOLD ME HER COUSIN'S BEEN MOLESTING HER FOR SIX SUMMERS NOW.

AIN'T YOU, UH . . .

HE GETS HERE IN THREE DAYS. LET'S HAVE A SURPRISE FOR THE SON-OF-A-BITCH.

THE PART OF THEM THAT WANTED SOMETHIN' TO HAPPEN TO THEIR DADDY, THEIR COUSIN, BROTHER IN THE WORST WAY WAS LET LOOSE. A WOMAN'S HATE IS SMALL, BRIGHT AND WHITE-HOT AND IT CAN STAY THAT WAY FOR A LONG TIME, BECAUSE THEY CAN WORK AROUND IT. WHAT BECOMES GUILT IN A MAN BECOMES ENSHROUDED HATE IN A WOMAN.

WHAT WE SAW WAS A *RITUAL*, A RITUAL OF AWAKENING.

A WOMAN EXPRESSED HER HATE IN ITS SIMPLEST, MOST POWERFUL FORM AND THEY *I*-DENTIFIED.

I BET THEY SAW THIS START.

MRM!

CARLA.

JANINA.

LUCY ANNE.

JANETT.

PAMELA.

JUDY.

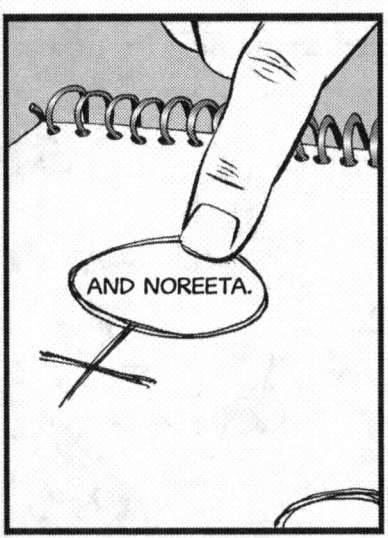

AND NOREETA.

THEY CAME OUT TO WATCH.

SEVEN WOMEN, SEVEN INTERPRETIVE DESCRIPTIONS.

SEVEN TARGETS IN THE LINE OF FIRE.

SEVEN BALLS OF HATE LOOKING FOR RELEASE.

EVEN IF THEY COULD NEVER HAVE ADMITTED AS MUCH BEFORE THE INCIDENT.

THEY ARE *NEVER* GONNA FINGER HER IN COURT.

THE OTHERS' LL HAVE HELPFUL OBSERVATIONS LIKE

*"LOUD NOISE, TALL, WHITE CLOTHES."*

OH, MAN, YOU' RE RIGHT. I JUST WANNA *THUMP* DYLAN FOR THIS.

AAH. HE' S ALL THE WAY ACROSS TOWN.

YEAH. SO YOU WANNA CHARGE ANY OF 'EM?

FOR ACCESSORY?

YEAH. MIGHT LOOSEN SOME TONGUES.

THEY COULD NEVER HAVE STOPPED HER.

THERE WAS NO PLAN HERE.

SO HOW IS IT THAT SEVEN OF THESE WOMEN JUST HAPPEN TO BE VICTIMS OF SEXUAL ABUSE?

YOU MISSED DINNER, BUT YOU'RE OH-SO-WELCOME TO DIVE INTO A SHAKE WITH US.

I THOUGHT MAYBE YOU TWO DIDN'T LIKE ME VERY MUCH.

LOOKS LIKE WE'RE NOT GONNA FIND ANY OF YOUR FINGERPRINTS ON ANY OF IT.

WE *LOVE* YOU.

EVEN THOUGH THE OTHERS DID TOUCH STUFF?

I MEAN, I DIDN'T KNOW ENOUGH TO STOP 'EM.

YOUR PEERS GOT MOMENTUM, DEPUTY: FIRST RULE OF CROWDS.

WHAT'S TICKLING YA?

NOREETA.

*NO*-REETA.

WHAT IS NOREETA UP TO?

SHE DEMANDED HER ONE PHONE CALL.

SHE AIN'T UNDER ARREST.

I EXPLAINED THAT TO HER.

LATE CITY FINAL
FREEDOM CITY 25
FREEDOM CITY 25

# FREEDOM CITY JOURNAL

**25 CENTS**

**LATE CITY FINAL**

# "I DID IT FOR MY ANGEL"

## "I will kill until he comes-- I will not wait."

09x15x53

**A JOURNAL EXCLUSIVE**

Freedom City has a new menace, and her name is the MADONNA! Twelve men lie dead in her wake, riddled with bullets. What does the MADONNA want? One man: THE NIGHT ANGEL! In an exclusive interview with the JOURNAL, a witness to the carnage at FIVE CORNERS MALL has revealed the true purpose behind this horror: LOVE OF AN ANGEL. What will the NIGHT ANGEL do? Is he pulling the strings?

ROSCO DRUG

FULL STORY: PAGE 4

THAT CAN CHANGE.
WHAT?
HAVE A BATH, THEN PUT IT ON. YOU'RE COVERED IN DROOL.
WHAT ABOUT THE ANGEL?
HE'LL BE OUR FRIEND. HE'S LOST HIS WAY RIGHT NOW.
WE CHANGE HIM.
WE CHANGE HIM.
I HATE IT WHEN WE FIGHT.
THE NAVY TEACHES SOME TIGHT KNOTS.
Knock
I WAS IN THE NAVY?
YES.
HOW DO YOU KNOW THAT?
Knock
KNOCK
IT'S MY JOB TO KNOW THESE THINGS.
Knock
Knock
Knock

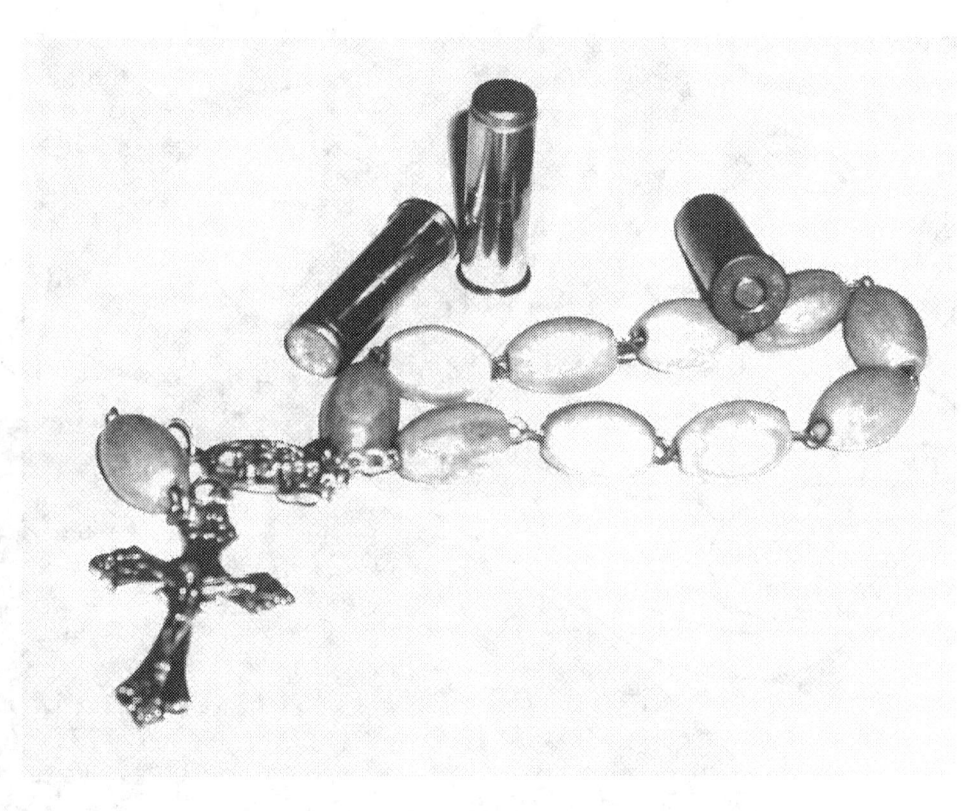

WONDERFUL.

A MEANINGLESS HOLDUP.

WHAT WERE THE FEARSOME SHADE AND THE NIGHT ANGEL THINKING?

SORT OUT WHAT HAPPENED.

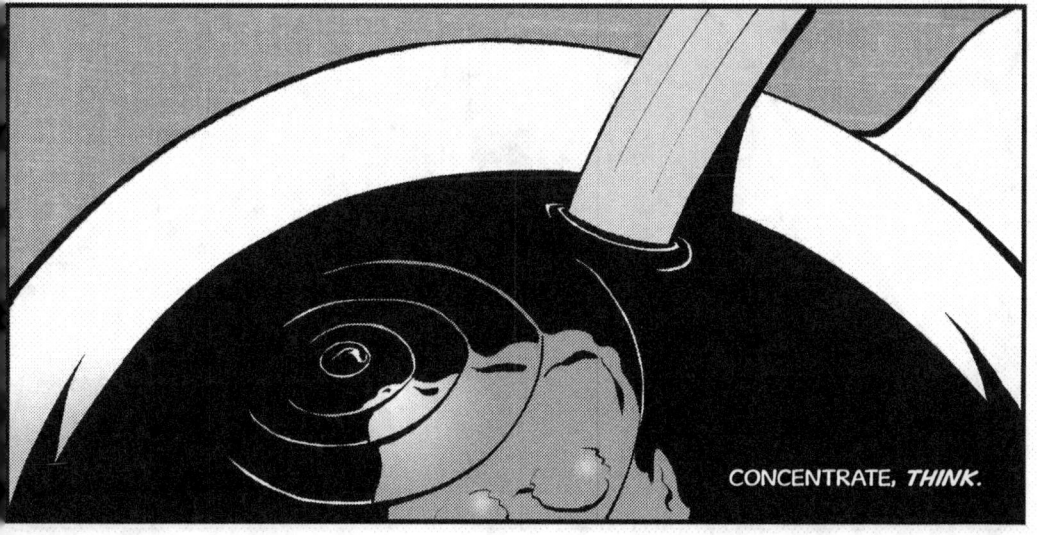

CONCENTRATE, *THINK*.

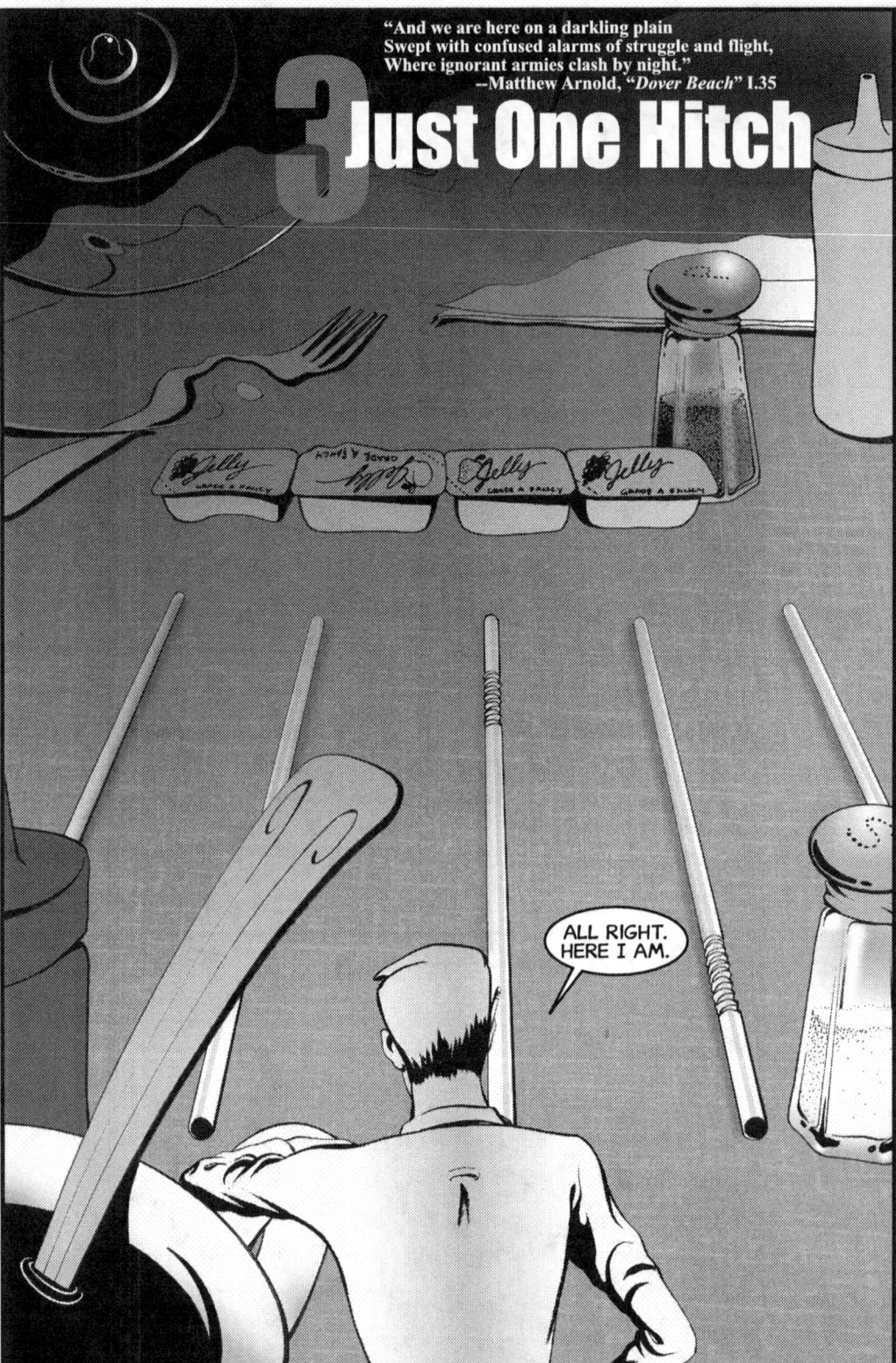

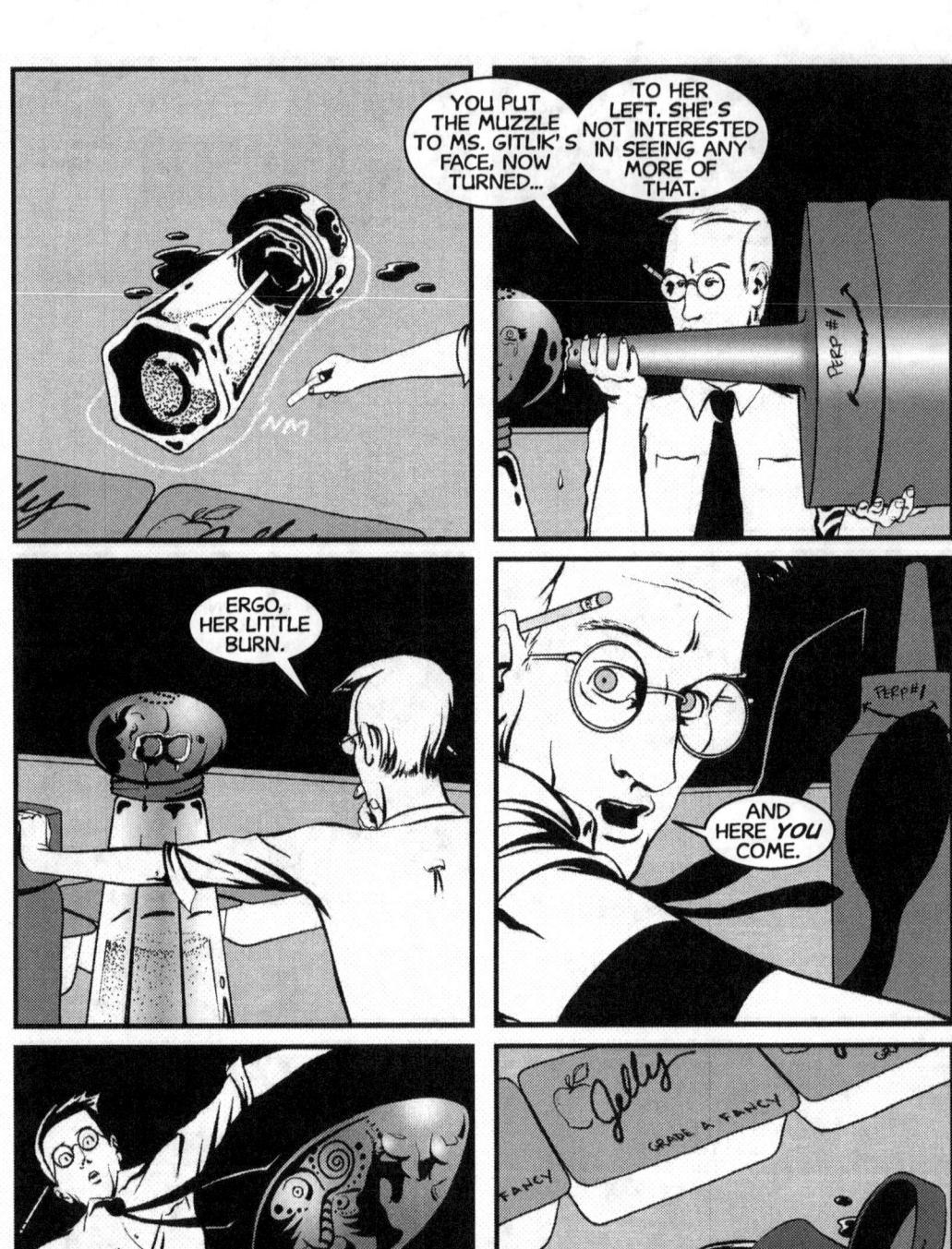

HEY, NAT.

YOU'RE NOT WAITING FOR THE EGGS TO FINISH THIS LITTLE DIORAMA, ARE YOU?

ROSCO DRUG HOLDUP STILL ON YOUR MIND?

THAT'S A WEEK OLD, NAT. EVEN THE FEARSOME SHADE IS PAST IT.

RIGHT NOW, AT THE CULMINATION OF 24 HOURS OF MALFEASANCE,

WE'VE GOT A PILE OF BODIES WITH MORE HOLES THAN A DOUBLE FEATURE AT THE PORNUCOPIA.

MORE TONIGHT, AND TOMORROW, AND TOMORROW.

THE ORDER OF THINGS STAYS THE SAME--BREAKFAST, LUNCH, DINNER.

FRED AND TOM HAVE PROBABLY MANAGED TO FIND A LACTOSE KING BY THEIR INBRED CHOLESTEROL-SENSOR TECHNOLOGY.

DAN AND ARTY, SINCE IT'S THURSDAY, ARE HAVING CALZONES.

ALL DONE THERE?

MM-HM.

HARRY TRUMAN USED TO CONDUCT ALL FOREIGN VISITS AND BUSINESS BY EASTERN TIME, NO MATTER WHERE HE WAS.

WHAT DO THEIR SHIFT-ENDING MEALS SAY ABOUT THEM?

I DUNNO. THEY'RE HUNGRY. NOT WRITING A NEW AGE BOOK HERE.

WHERE ARE YOU?

WHY ARE YOU LEAVING ME IN THE DARK, FEARSOME SHADE?

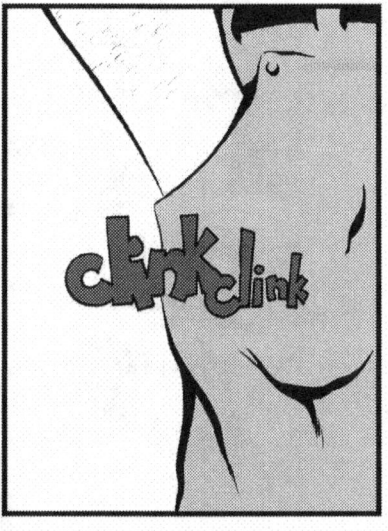

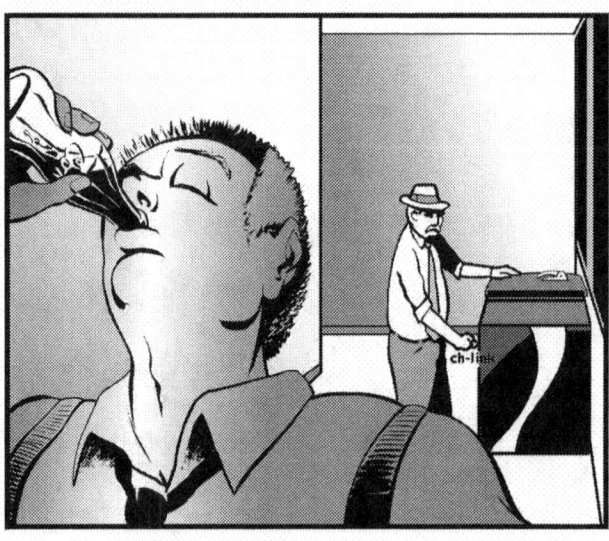

THESE WOMEN ARE *PISSING* ME OFF, NOW.

HATE MEN?

HATE *WOMEN!*

NOW IT'S ALL THOSE MEN WERE ASKING FOR IT WITH A LEER, *ASKING* FOR A *DATE*, LITTLE STUFF.

NOW THEY SEE THE BLOOD ON THE DRESS.

THEY'RE TRYIN' TO UNDERSTAND THIS MADONNA.

MINDS ARE CATCHIN' UP WITH WHAT HAPPENED, SEE.

NOT LONG BEFORE THEY STOP TALKIN' POETRY AND START TALKIN' ABOUT PLACES WITH RIGHT ANGLES AND SOLID SIDES.

*GOD,* I REALLY...

TOM.

TOM CAME OUT OF SPECIAL WEAPONS AND TACTICS.

I SAY THE WHOLE THING 'CAUSE SWAT'S A WORD THAT'S OVERUSED, DOESN'T BRING ACROSS THE IDEA OF WHAT THESE GUYS LEARN TO DO.

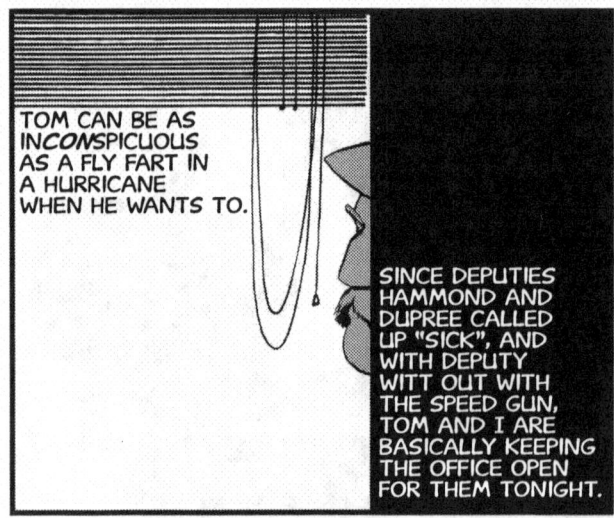

TOM CAN BE AS IN*CON*SPICUOUS AS A FLY FART IN A HURRICANE WHEN HE WANTS TO.

SINCE DEPUTIES HAMMOND AND DUPREE CALLED UP "SICK", AND WITH DEPUTY WITT OUT WITH THE SPEED GUN, TOM AND I ARE BASICALLY KEEPING THE OFFICE OPEN FOR THEM TONIGHT.

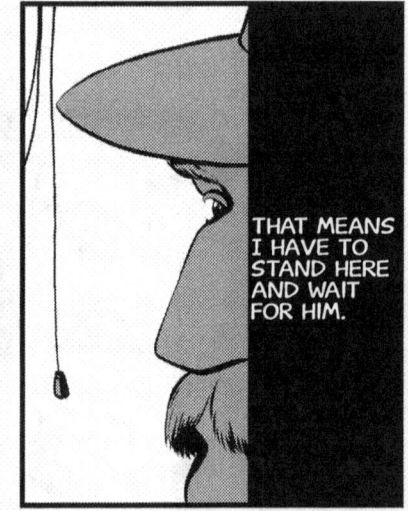

THAT MEANS I HAVE TO STAND HERE AND WAIT FOR HIM.

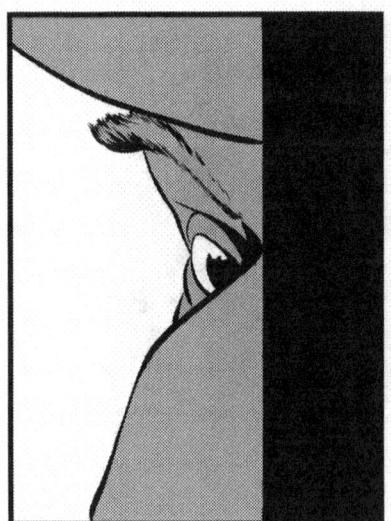

DEPUTY WITT, REQUEST YOU COME HOME FOR A SPELL, BASE CLEAR.

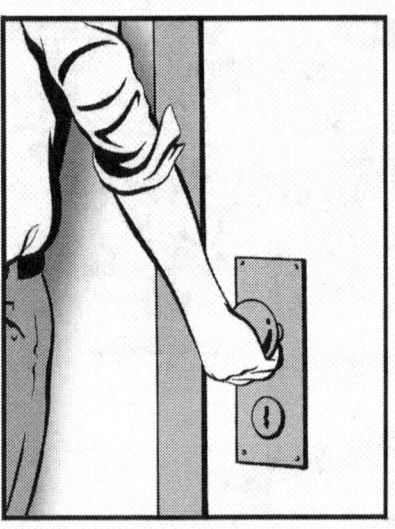

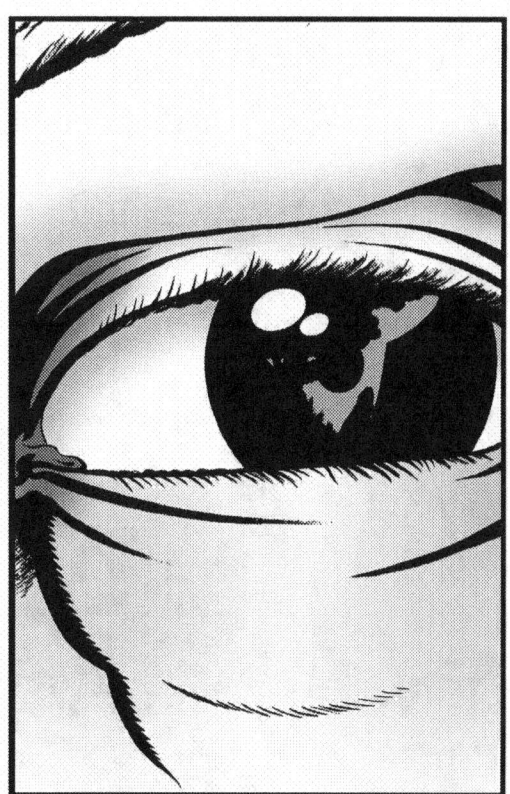
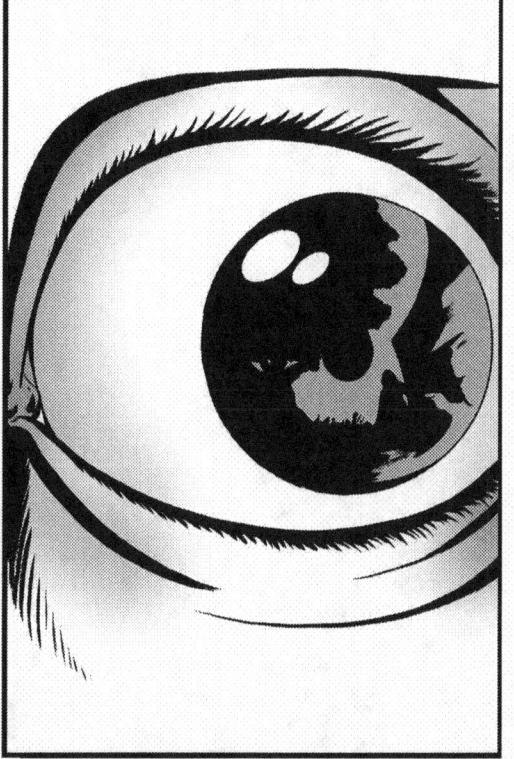

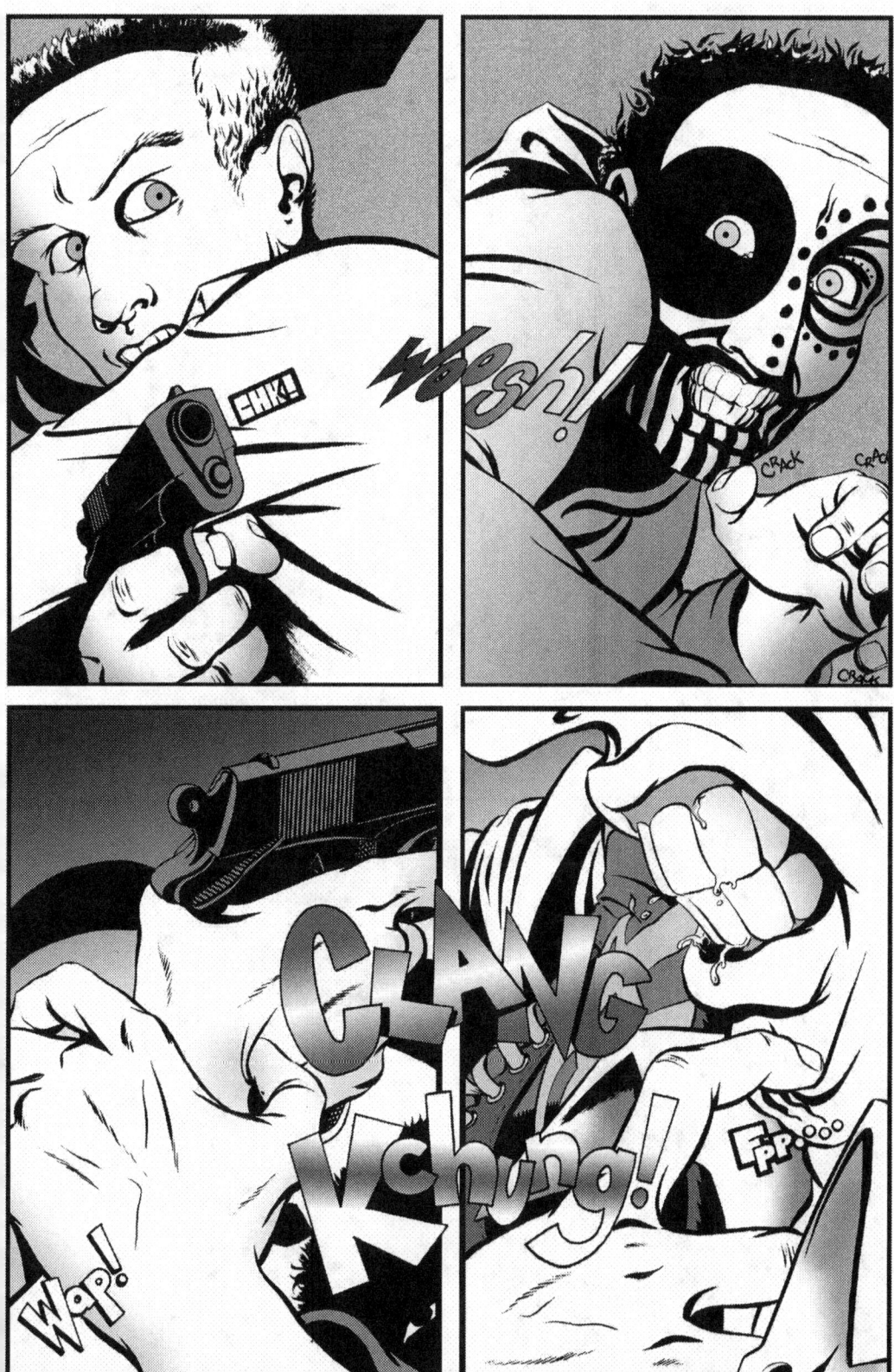

# 4 Bait And Switch

"What do you feel when our bones crunch, you hear them, between your teeth?
when your fingers break our ribs?
when you see naked heart steaming in your palm?"
--Vizma Belsevica, "*Painting Signatures*"

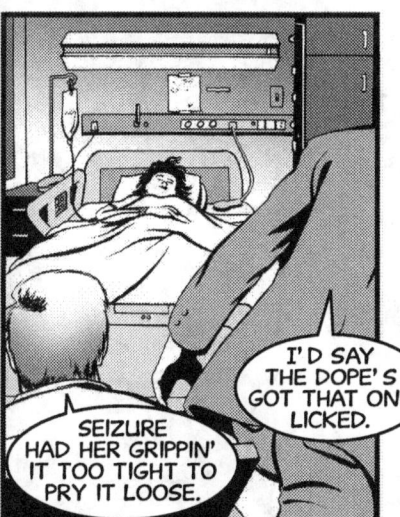

GIVE HERE.

SOME KINDA OIL, MAYBE? SEALED ALL 'ROUND.

LIKE A BIG FLOPPY BATH BEAD.

BATH BEAD?

SQUISH 'EM IN THE TUB FOR THE OIL IN 'EM.

DECORATIVE THINGS.

PUT 'EM IN JARS ABOVE THE TOILET.

TOMMY, YOU WAS ALL THE *WAY* MARRIED, WEREN'T YA?

HEH!

HAH!

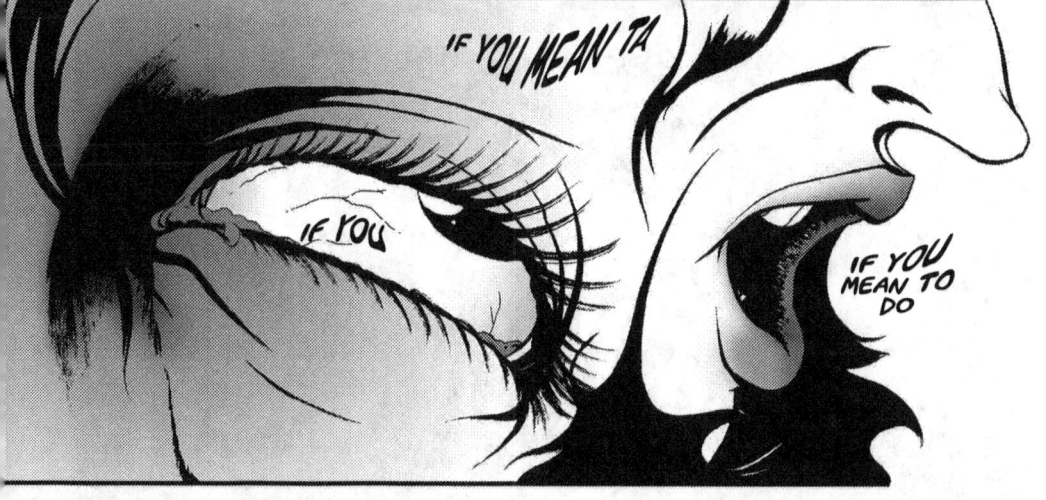

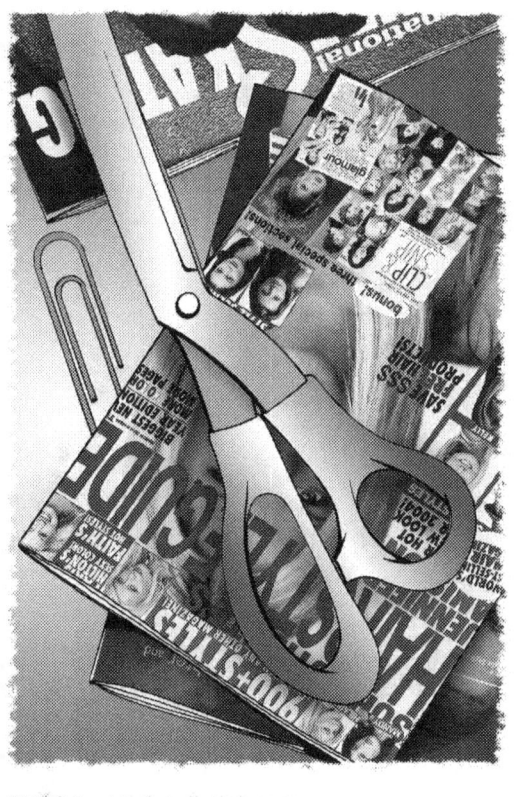

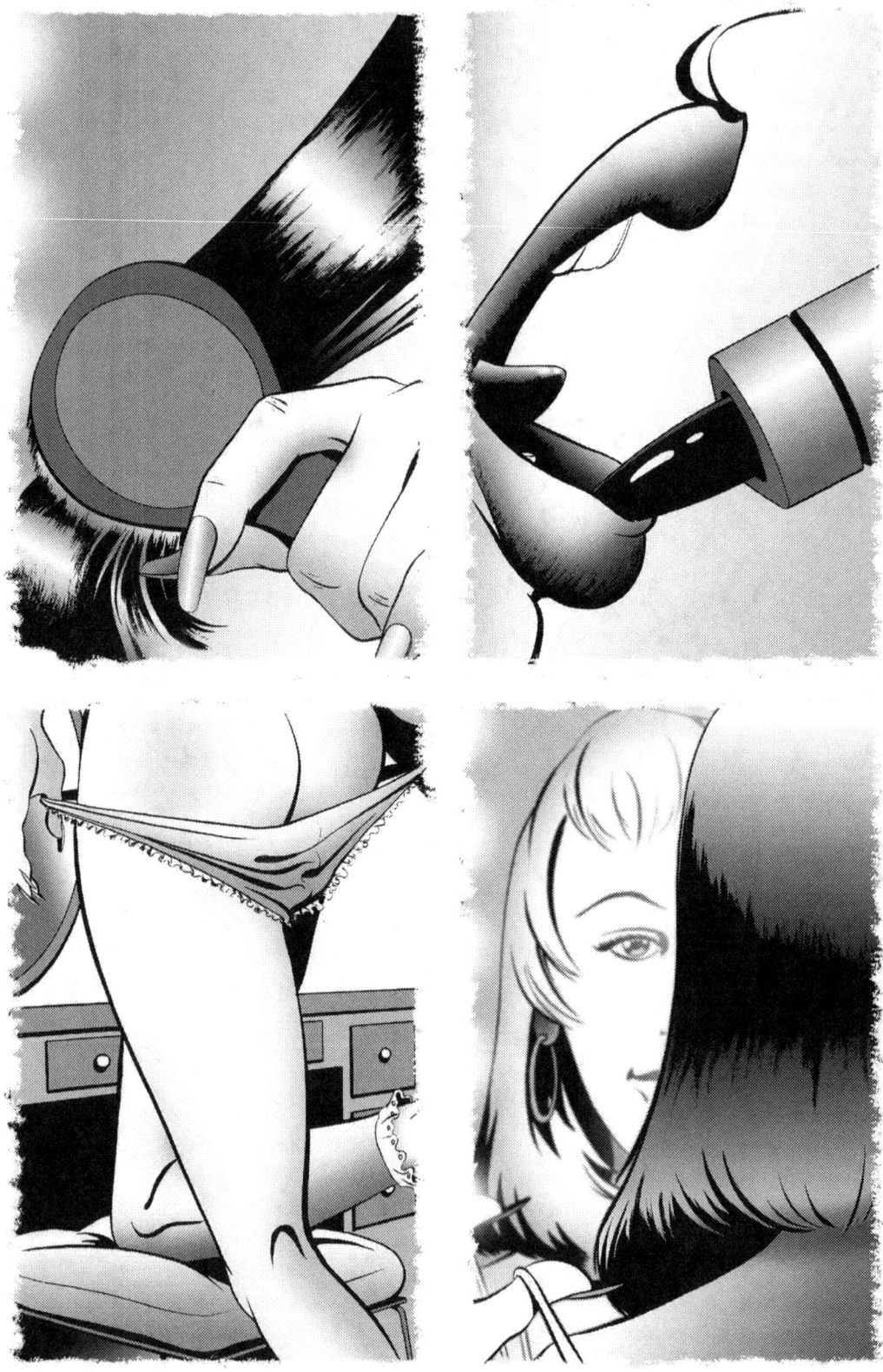

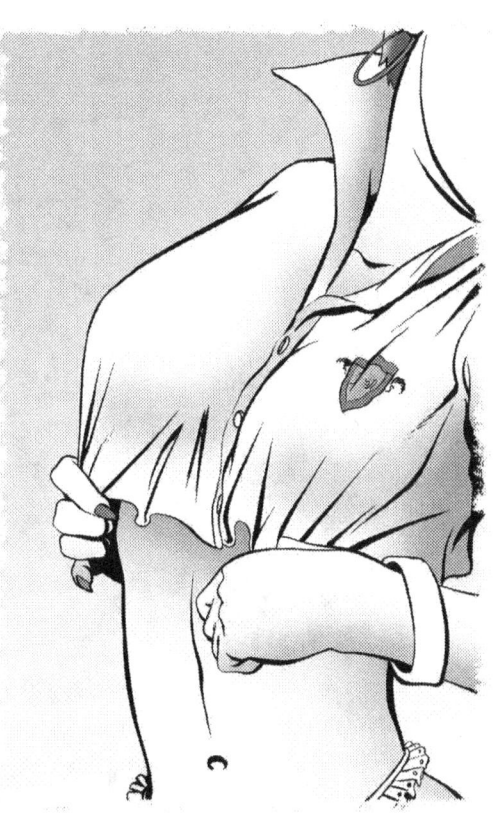
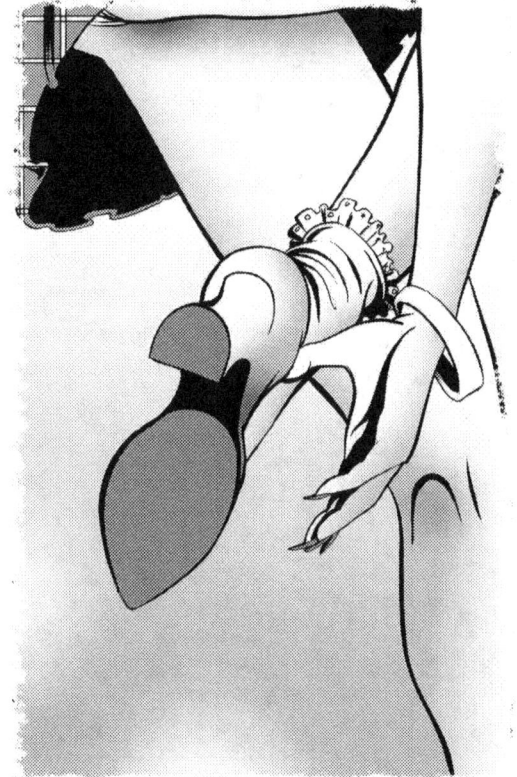

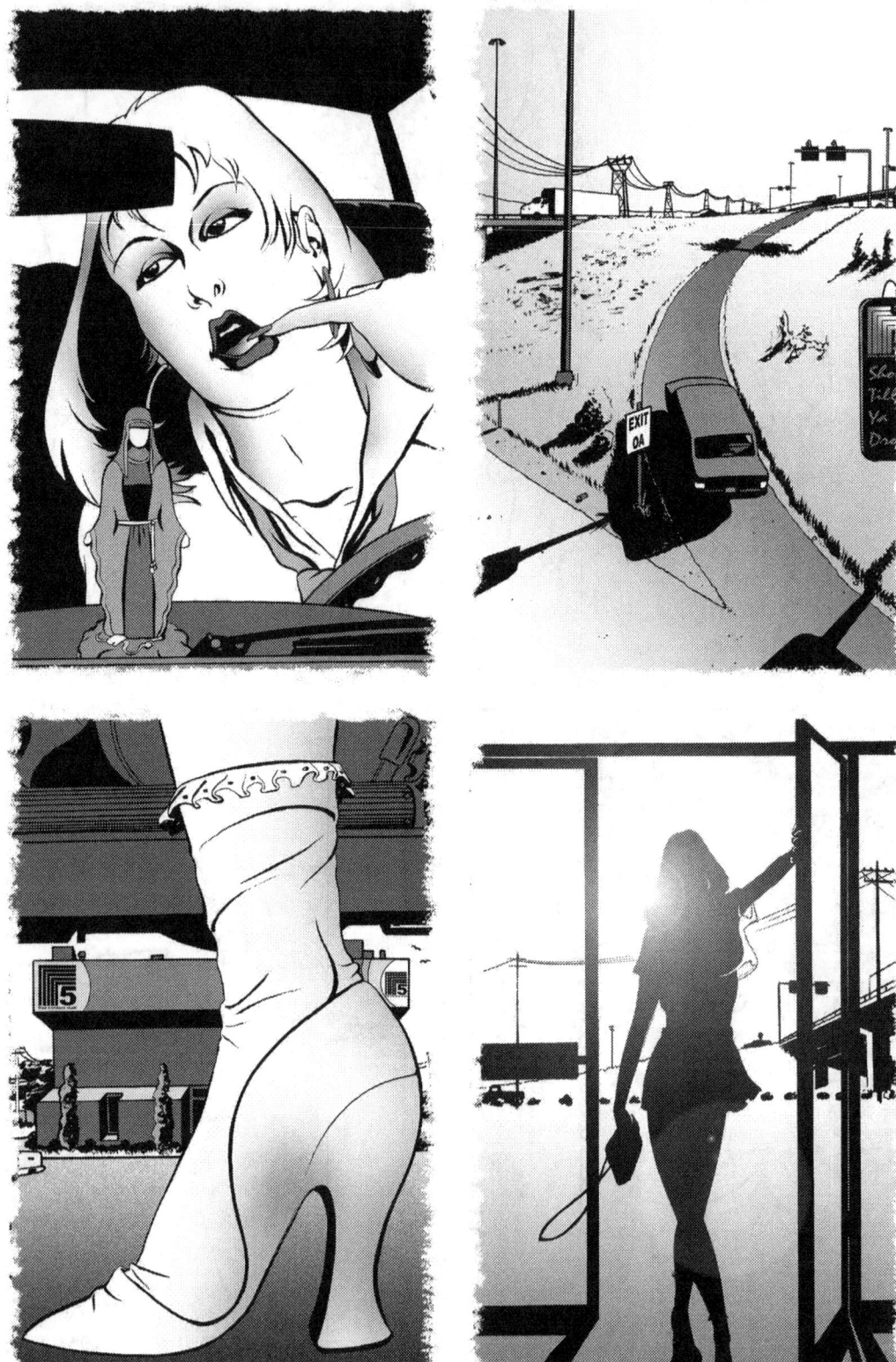

Zip!

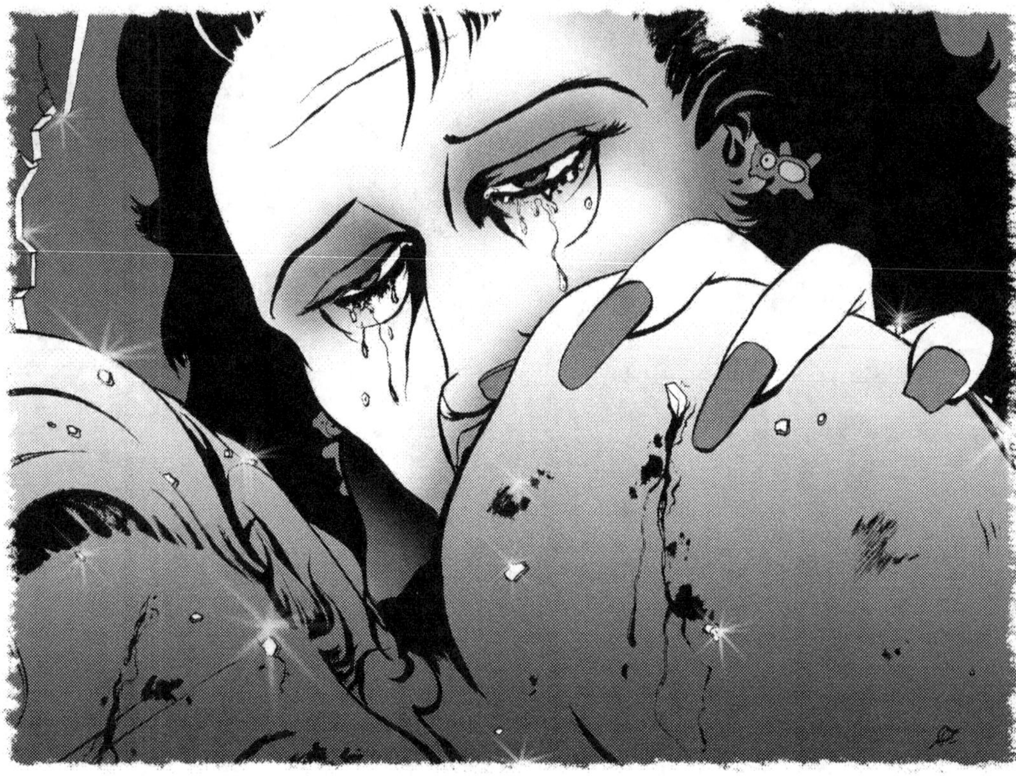

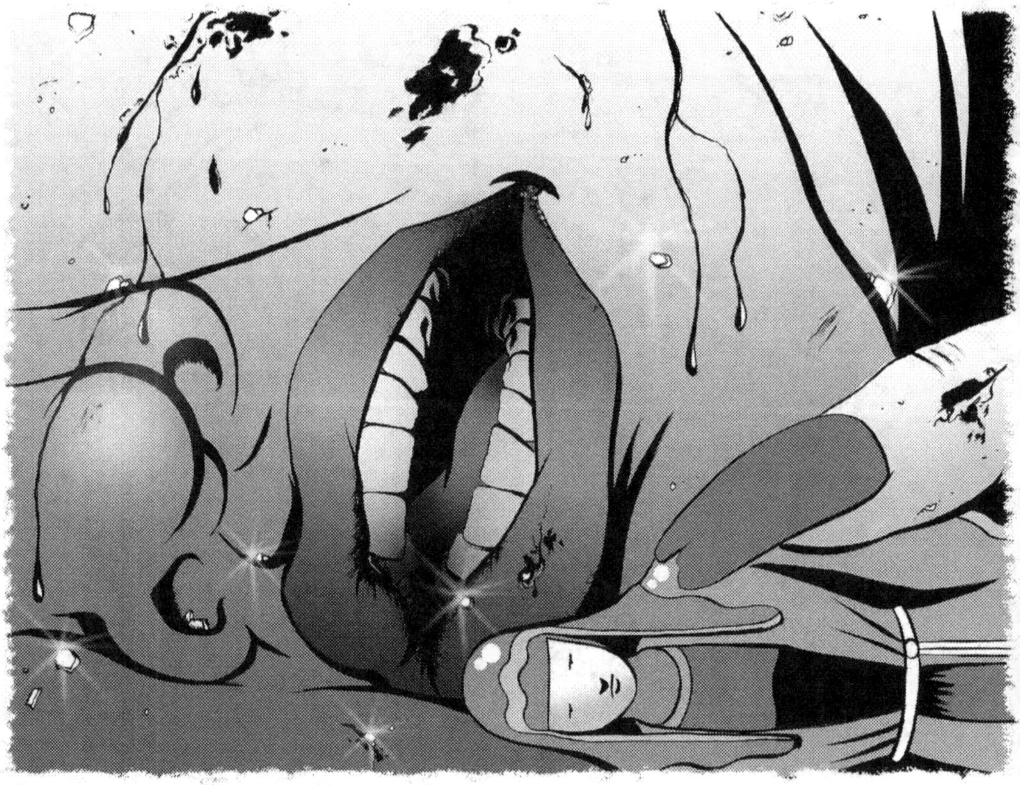

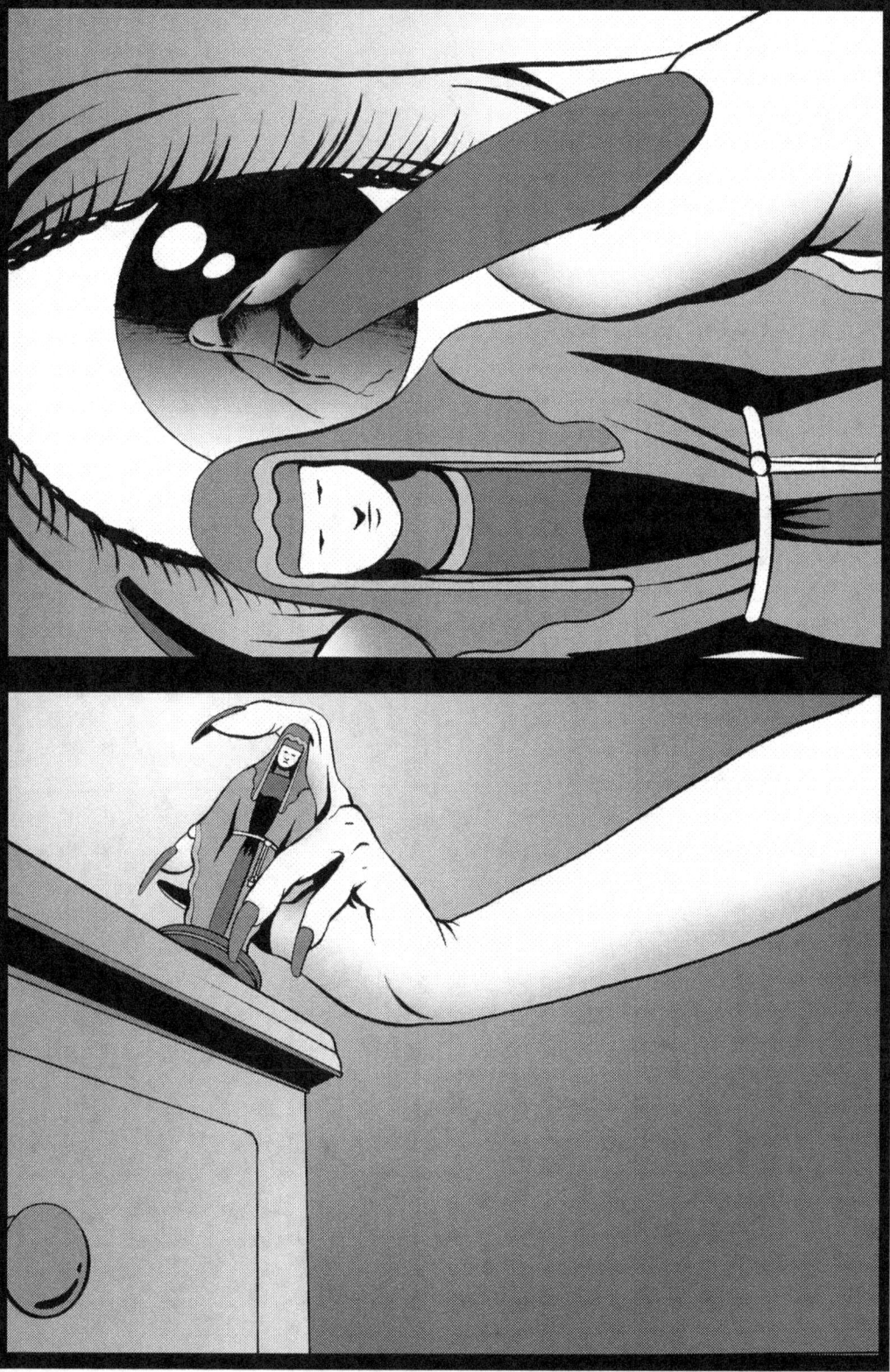

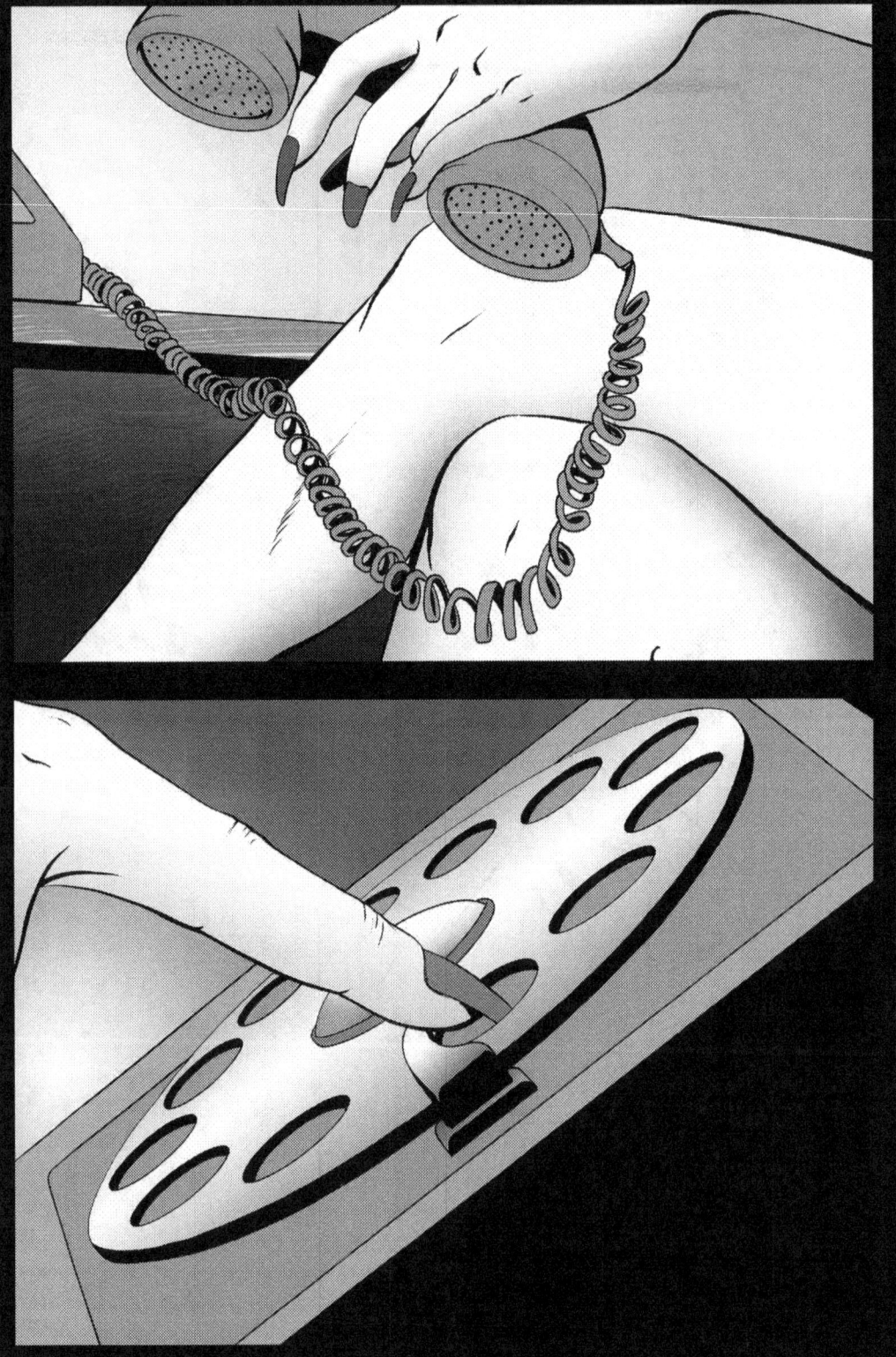

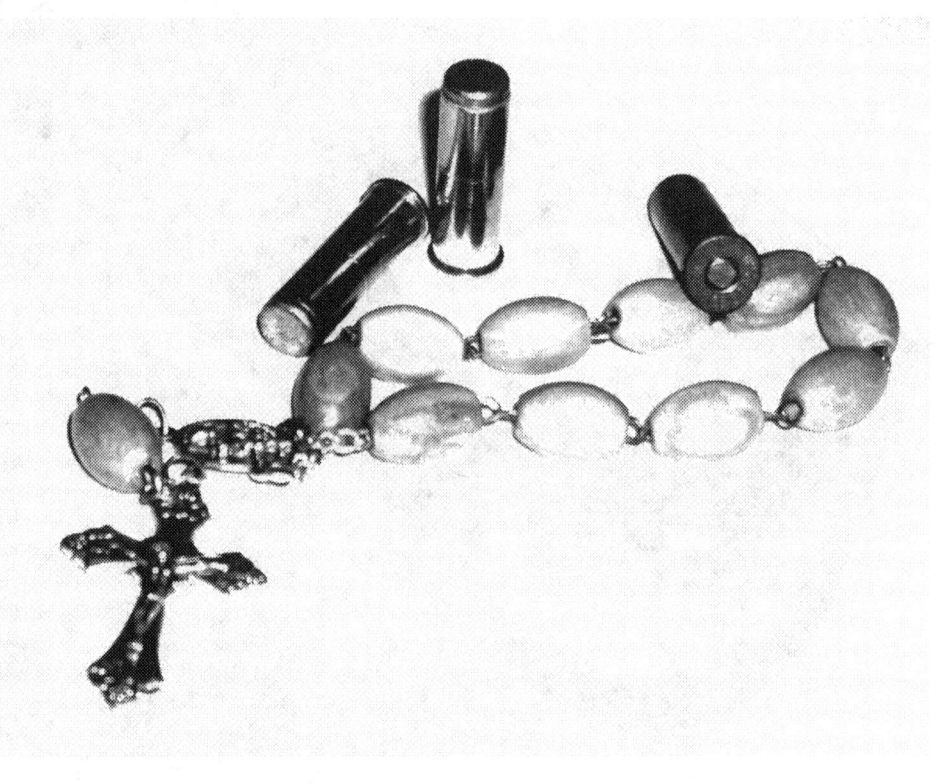

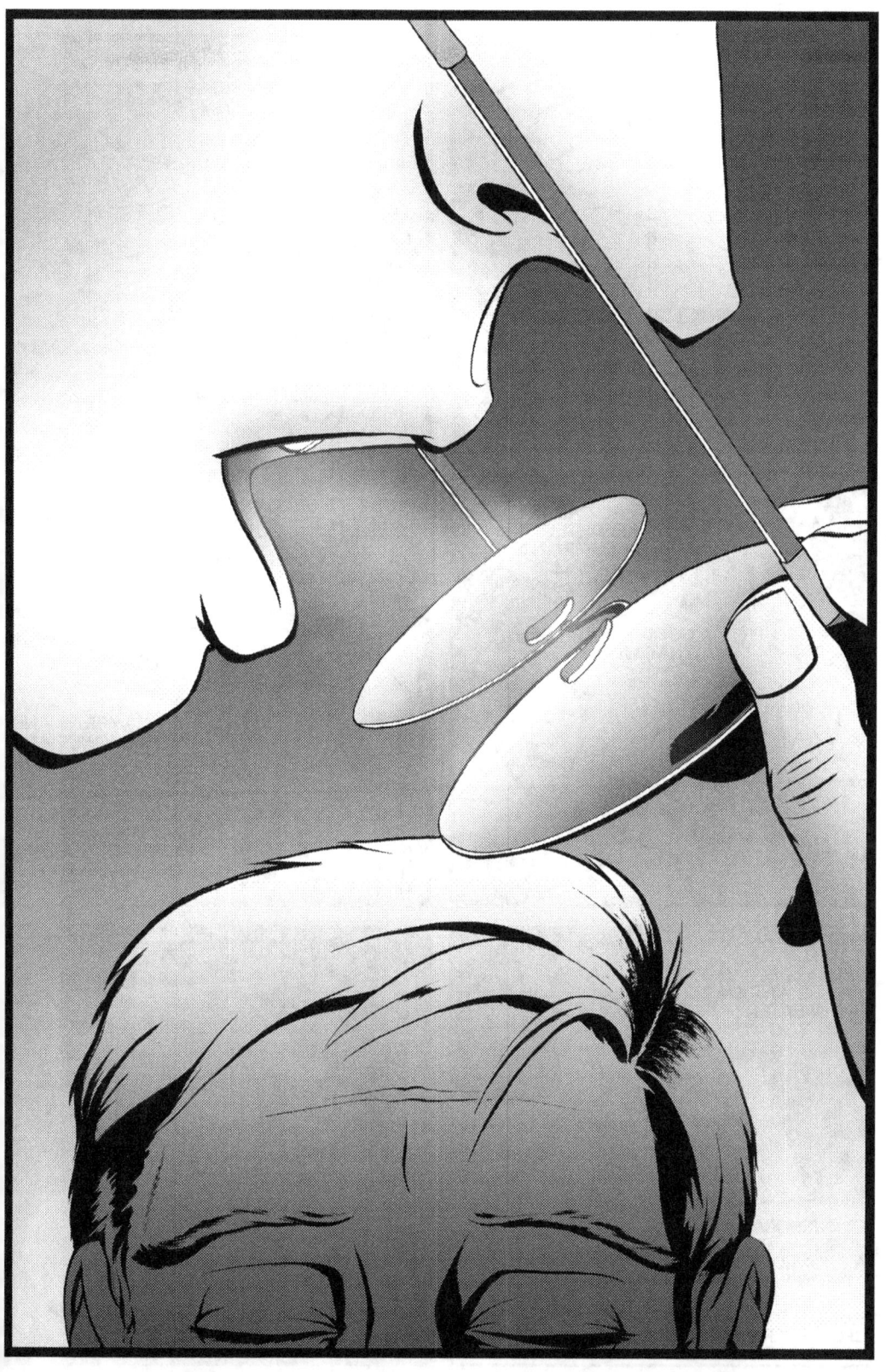

SERGEANT. WE MISSED ROLL CALL?

UNDERSTANDABLY.

DEPUTY WITT!

HE CAUGHT ME, DETECTIVE. HE'S IN THE HALL.

GOOD BOY, THAT WITT

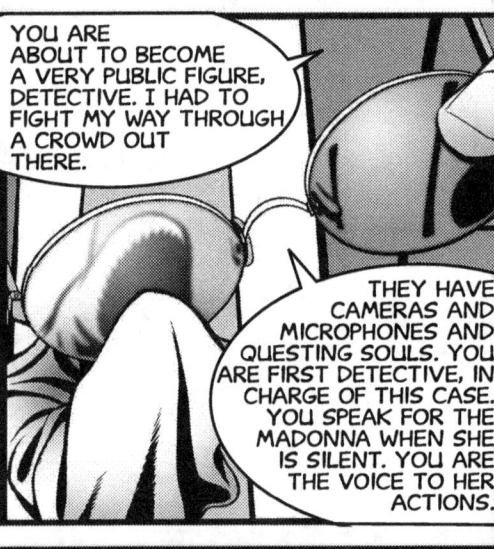

YOU ARE ABOUT TO BECOME A VERY PUBLIC FIGURE, DETECTIVE. I HAD TO FIGHT MY WAY THROUGH A CROWD OUT THERE.

THEY HAVE CAMERAS AND MICROPHONES AND QUESTING SOULS. YOU ARE FIRST DETECTIVE, IN CHARGE OF THIS CASE. YOU SPEAK FOR THE MADONNA WHEN SHE IS SILENT. YOU ARE THE VOICE TO HER ACTIONS.

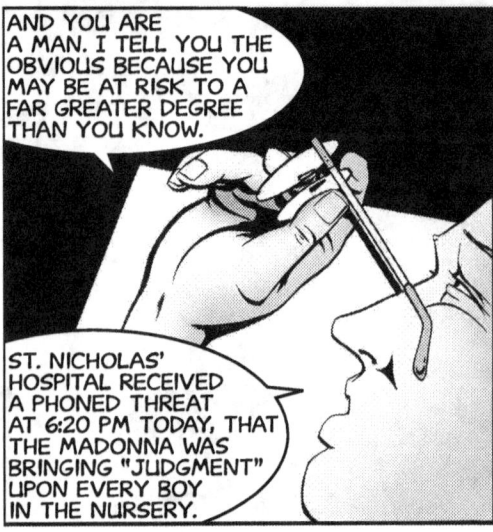

AND YOU ARE A MAN. I TELL YOU THE OBVIOUS BECAUSE YOU MAY BE AT RISK TO A FAR GREATER DEGREE THAN YOU KNOW.

ST. NICHOLAS' HOSPITAL RECEIVED A PHONED THREAT AT 6:20 PM TODAY, THAT THE MADONNA WAS BRINGING "JUDGMENT" UPON EVERY BOY IN THE NURSERY.

THE CALL WAS STAR-SIX-NINED BACK TO THE HOME OF AN O.B. NURSE WITH A SHIFT IN NURSERY TONIGHT.

SHE HAVE A HISTORY OF BEING ABUSED?

SHE WAS STILL DETAILING IT WHEN I LEFT. IT IS ALL SHE WISHES TO TALK ABOUT.

DAMN.

ASSAULT AND DOMESTIC DISTURBANCE CALLS HAVE DOUBLED OVER THE LAST 48 HOURS.

SEXUAL CRIMES HAS A LINE OF WOMEN EXTENDING INTO THE STREET.

RAPE CRISIS HOTLINES ARE JAMMED.

THE WOMEN OF FREEDOM CITY SEEK TO UNBURDEN THEMSELVES.

EXPIATE.

THEY'VE COMMITTED NO SIN.

SILENCE. SILENCE IS A SIN.

WHAT TOUCHED OFF THE FUSE?

YOU *KNOW* NOREETA'S STORY.

Y' READ IT, HELL THE FEARSOME *SHADE* READ IT, IN THE PAPER.

TODAY HAD MOST OF THE REST OF OUR WITNESSES' STORIES, TOO.

THE MEDIA OFTEN CARRY SUCH STORIES.

SEVEN, ALL AT ONCE, WITNESSES TO MARY MOTHER OF JESUS STRIKING DOWN TWELVE MEN OUT IN THE BOONIES?

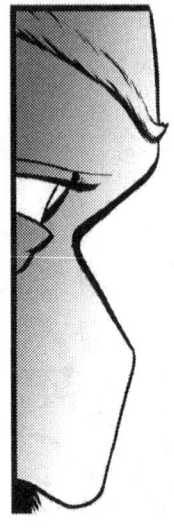

Y' DON'T HAVE TO *EXPLAIN* A RITUAL TO PEOPLE WHO ALREADY KNOW WHAT ISSUES ARE AT STAKE. HAVE YOU THOUGHT ABOUT WHAT ALL THIS SAYS, SYMBOLICALLY? IT SAYS TO ME: WOMAN GAVE US SALVATION, IN EXACTLY THE WAY WE WANTED IT, IN A MAN'S FORM, AND LOOK WHAT HAPPENED. SO NOW SHE USES THE FAILINGS OF MAN TO DESTROY US, TO MAKE A POINT.

WE KILLED MARY'S SON; AND NOW THERE SHALL BE NO MORE SONS.

SHE CANNOT DO THAT; IT IS COMPLETELY UNFEASIBLE.

WHO YOU TELLIN'?

IT'S ALL VERY CONFUSING.

COULD JUST BE COINCIDENCE, WORLDWIDE ATTACK OF PMS, HIGH TIDES.

BUT I'LL KEEP MY EYES OPEN IN CASE SOMEBODY DECIDES T' TAKE AN ACTIVE ROLE IN KEEPING THE MADONNA FREE.

I WOULD ALSO APPRECIATE IT IF YOU DID NOT MENTION THE FEARSOME SHADE TO THE MEDIA.

I APPRECIATE THE WARNING.

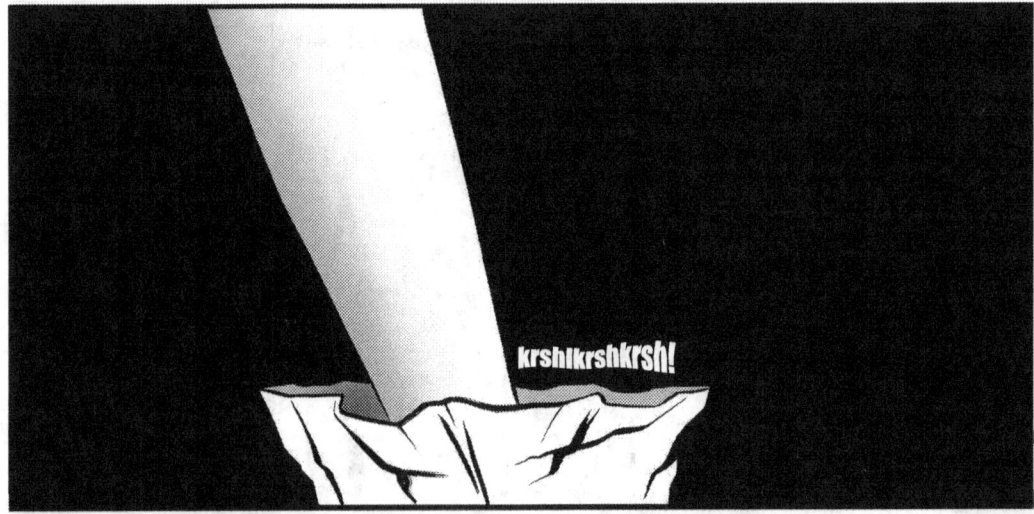

# Can't Say Which

**5**

"She who trifles with all
Is less likely to fall
Than she who but trifles with one."
--John Gay, *"The Coquette Mother
and Daughter"*

IT JUST MOVED UP AN INCOME BRACKET ALLA SUDDEN.

I'VE PULLED FIVE, SIX BABIES FROM DUMPSTERS IN TEN OR SO YEARS. KIDS WERE JUST TRASH TO THEM.

CITY LIVING. CAN'T BURY A BODY IN ASPHALT.

CITY'S GOT A TOUGH OUTER SHELL FOR SURE.

SO...

SO...

WE'RE DOING A SHOW ON THE MADONNA KILLINGS IN THREE DAYS.

SHE DEAD? ALWAYS LIKED THOSE VIDEOS.

YOU WANNA GET FED AGAIN?

LITTLE OUT OF MY EXPERIENCE, RITA; I APPEAR NOT TO BE AMONG THE PRECIOUS FEW WHO'VE HAD TO PICK UP AFTER HER.

YOU'RE OUR MAN IN HOMICIDE.

ASK ME AGAIN WHEN I'M HUNGRY.

SHE DOESN'T INTEREST YOU MUCH, DOES SHE?

HAVE TO HAVE PRIORITIES.

YOU DON'T THINK SHE'S ALL THAT IMPORTANT, HUH?

THRILL-KILLER, FAST ON HER FEET, NO SPECIFIC BONES TO PICK.

IT'S NOT "MUST KILL TOM AND DICK, DON'T CARE ABOUT HARRY".

ACTUALLY, IT'S MORE LIKE... "JUST KILL DICK".

HA.

HA.

SHE GETS IN THE MOOD AND THAT'S IT.

OH, SHE MEANS SOMETHING A LOT LARGER THAN THAT.

SEE, WE'RE EMPOWERED IN A NEW WAY NOW.

WE HAVE OUR OWN FEARSOME SHADE NOW, KILLING ALL THOSE NAS-TY MEN.

KILLING AN AWFUL LOT OF NICE MEN, TOO.

EVEN THE FEARSOME SHADE'S NOT A HUNDRED PERCENT.

ESPECIALLY NOT THE FEARSOME SHADE.

FOR CHRISSAKES RITA--YOU BUY ME DIN-DINS AND EXPECT ME TO LISTEN TO MADNESS?

CALL-IN TIME.

WILL YOU BE ON?

SURE. DYLAN HAD KITTENS WHEN I WENT ON A SHOW ABOUT THE FEARSOME SHADE.

I'M SURE HE'LL BE QUITE HAPPY THAT I'M BROADENING MY INTERESTS.

ON AIR

SURE THERE WON'T BE ANY CRIME THEN?

MY INTERIM PARTNER'S GOT A PREVIOUS ENGAGEMENT THEN.

HE'S, AH, GOING TO HIS DAUGHTER'S PROM, CHAPERONING.

OH, CHAPERONING'S SO SWEET. WHY ARE YOU LAUGHING?

I'M JUST WONDERING WHAT'S GONNA HAPPEN TO GET HIM IN TROUBLE WITH HIS WIFE *THIS* TIME. I'M IN.

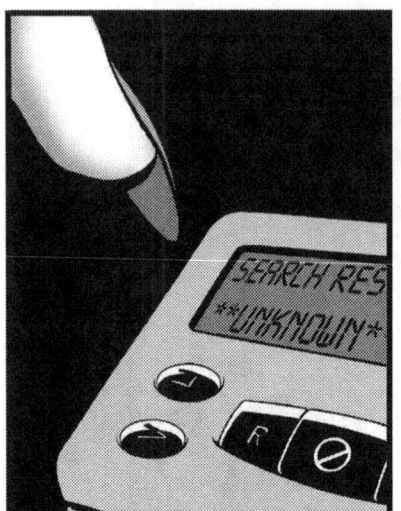

SHE'S BACK IN THE STICKS, THEN.

ANNELLE, WE HAVE THE MADONNA ON THE LINE.

SHE WANTS TO TALK ABOUT LOVE.

STUART CONFIRMS SHE'S THE REAL DEAL.

clix TCH..

YOU WANT HER BUSY FOR THREE MINUTES, THERE IT IS.

AGUERRO, I NEED A TRACE AUTHORIZED.

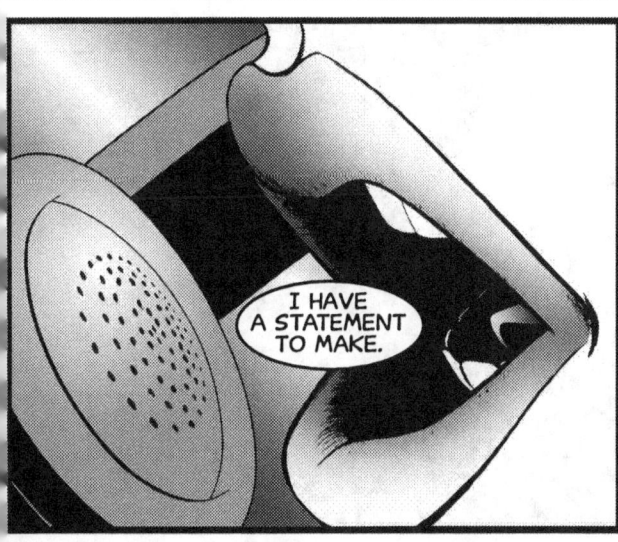

OKAY, GOOD; NOT THE *DAY* ANGEL, THEN.

ANNIE I'M KILLING MIKES 2 AND 3 AND PUTTING THE NIGHT ANGEL THROUGH TOO.

WHAT IS *THIS* ABOUT?

ON AIR

HELLO.

I AM . . . HELLO?

HELLO, CALLER.

HELLO.

YES, SIR. SOMETHING YOU'D LIKE TO SAY?

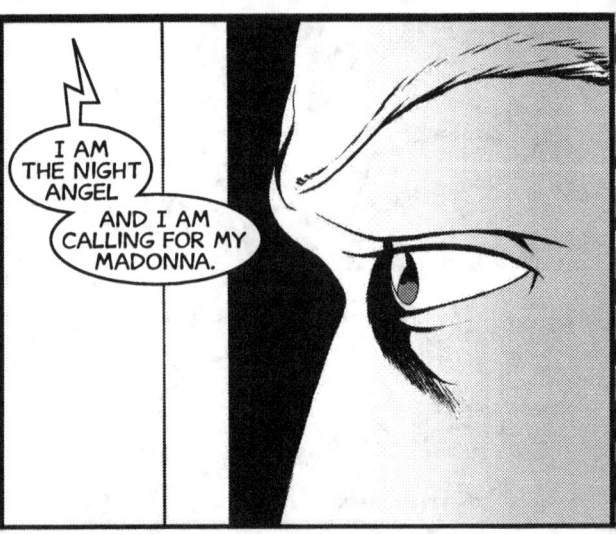

I AM THE NIGHT ANGEL

AND I AM CALLING FOR MY MADONNA.

SHADE.

IT'S THE FEARSOME SHADE.
NOT THE NIGHT ANGEL AT ALL.
YOU HAVE TO KILL MORE.

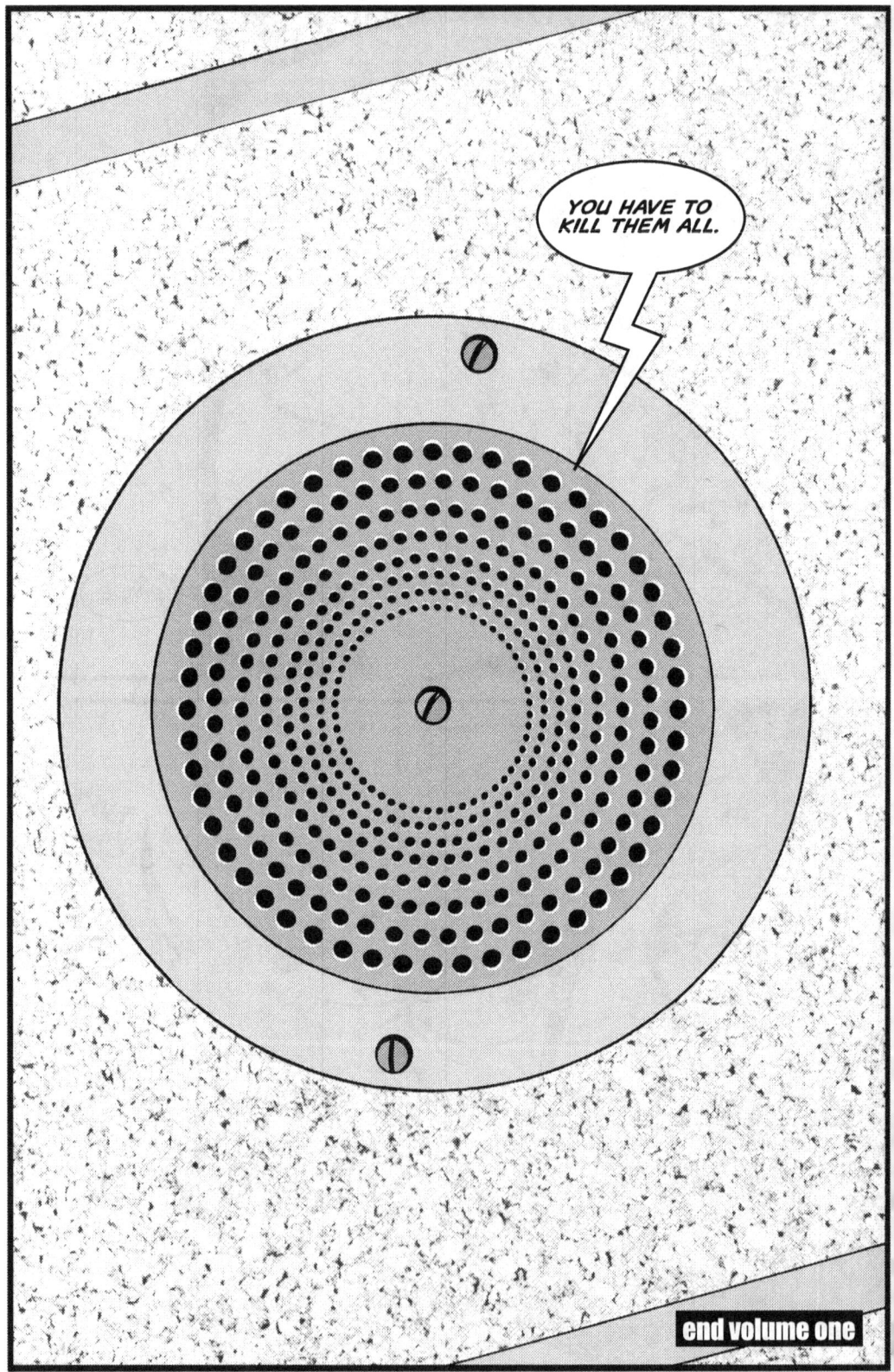

# Figure IV.18 Sketch Pad Showing Credits of Graphic Novel

## INJURY SYMBOLS

| IDENTIFYING MARKS | GUNSHOT WOUNDS | SHARP INSTRUMENT WOUNDS | BLUNT INJURY FORCE |
|---|---|---|---|
| (S) = Scar | (shotgun pellets) = Shotgun Pellets | (—) = Stab | (/) = Fracture- broken bones |
| (T) = Tattoo | (⊙) = Entrance | (═) = Incise - cut - slash | (⊗) = Laceration - tear |
| (D) = Deformity | (⊕) = Exit | (•) = Puncture(needle, nail, ice pick) | (⊗) = Fracture with laceration |
| | | | (═) = Abrasion-scrape-scratch |
| | | | (|||) = Contusion - bruise |

**BODY OF WORK DIAGRAM**
PRE AND POST PRODUCTION VIEWS

WORDS JOHN IRA THOMAS

PICTURES JEREMY SMITH

POST PRODUCTION ASSISTS CARTER ALLEN

LOVE AND SUPPORT DAVID & HANNA

PROOFS & CORRECTIONS HANNA, LISA, AND MIKE

MAY QUEEN FONT BY TOM MURPHY FONTS.TOM7.COM

EDDIE LIVES

BODY'S LENGTH 136 PAGES

SCALE 6.14×9.21

LOCATE EACH INJURY BY GIVING DISTANCE FROM TOP OF HEAD AND RIGHT OR LEFT OF MIDLINE

Graphic Novel (full name): THE FAIRER SEX: A TALE OF SHADES AND ANGELS VOLUME 1

Publisher: CANDLE LIGHT PRESS     Released: AUGUST, 2004     ISBN# 0-9743147-5-7

Place(s) Found: LOCAL BOOKSTORES, ONLINE BOOKSELLERS, COMICS SHOPS (VIA COLD CUT), LOCAL LIBRARIES

Copyright of Book, Art, Story, Characters, etc: © 2004 JOHN IRA THOMAS AND JEREMY SMITH

All Rights Reserved? YES     Country of First Publication: UNITED STATES OF AMERICA

Remarks: VOLUME TWO COMING 2005!

Website For Further Information: WWW.CANDLELIGHTPRESS.COM     WWW.THEFAIRERSEX.COM

Any other special markings:

Candle Light Press™

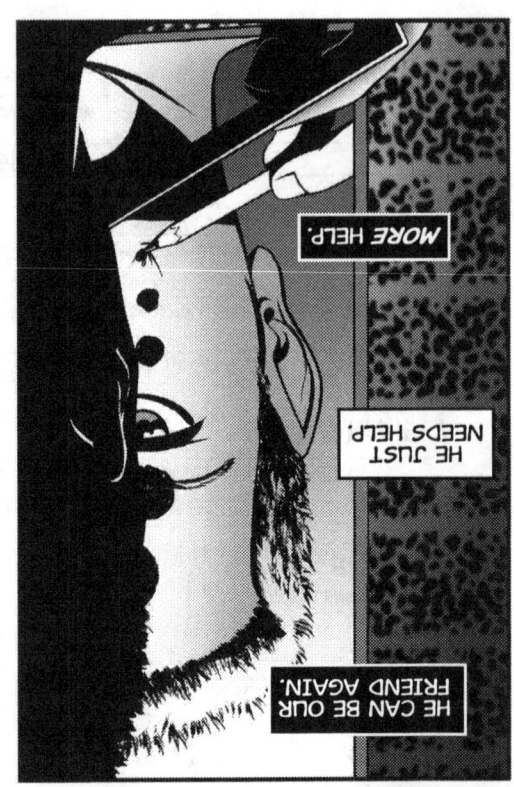

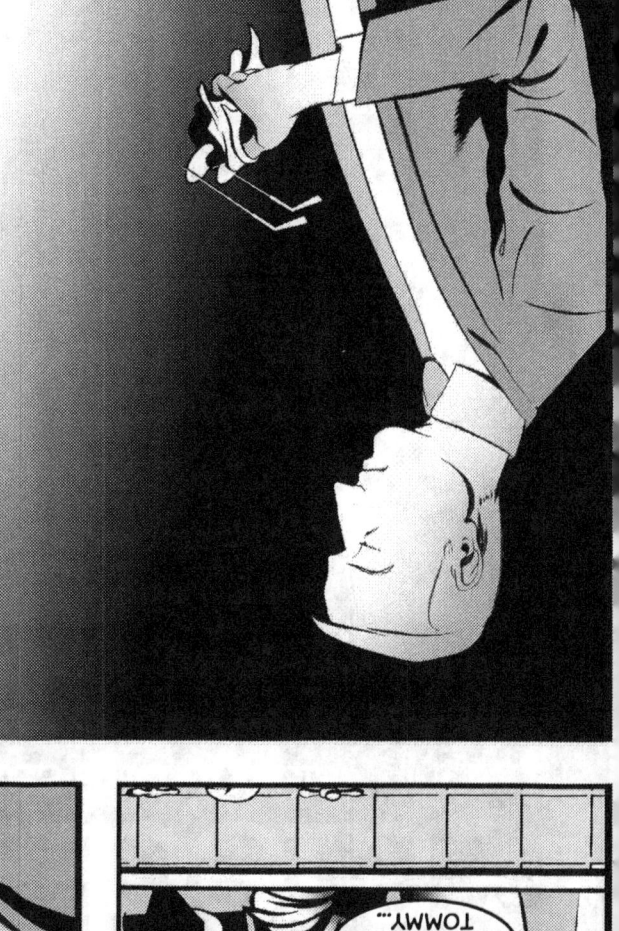

Candle Light Press

# the fairer sex: a tale of shades and angels

Volume Two
Coming 2005

by John Ira Thomas and Jeremy Smith

# numbers
## a tale of shades and angels

by John Ira Thomas & Jeremy Smith

paperback available wherever books are sold
(Order by ISBN Number 0-9743147-0-6)

www.ingramcontent.com/pod-product-compliance
Lightning Source LLC
Chambersburg PA
CBHW070600180626
46817CB00005B/1930